Patricia has left Waverley without a word of farewell to Tim Hardy.

Andy had assured her that he had done and said all that was necessary, but Patricia knew her uncle could not possibly have said everything to Tim that she had wanted to say. She pushed that disappointment back to the secret place deep within her where so much other sorrow was stored.

It seemed like the well of grief just kept getting fuller, deeper. Her mother. Her father. Danny disappearing the way he had. The change in Andy. And now Tim Hardy.

Patricia sat up a little straighter. Her lips settled in a tight, firm line. Those moments with Tim, that kiss, and her dreams had been a fantasy. There could be no future for the son of an English convict living in Australia and the daughter of Irish immigrants living in America.

She tried to brush the thoughts away, to concentrate on guiding the horse so he would not break a leg or tip the dray over on the uneven ground. But thoughts of the young man with the twinkling warm amber eyes who had strolled toward her across the sand on the Turon River, who had kissed her so tenderly with love and passion in his eyes would not be easily dismissed.

And Patricia had plenty of time for thinking.

MARY HAWKINS is an Australian married to a minister. They have two married sons, a daughter, and one grandson. Their ministry has taken them to many interesting places over the years. Besides almost forty years throughout Australia, these include Africa and even living for a few years in England trying to get used to those upside down seasons in a much colder climate! This is her eighth story for Heartsong Presents readers and the fourth in her Great Southland historical series.

Books by Mary Hawkins

Great Southland Gold

Mary Hawkins

Heartsong Presents

For Lois Bentley, a great sister-in-law, encourager, best friend, and one who shares my love of reading those romance novels!

A note from the author:
I love to hear from my readers! You may correspond with me by writing:

> **Mary Hawkins**
> **Author Relations**
> **PO Box 719**
> **Uhrichsville, OH 44683**

ISBN 1-58660-614-X

GREAT SOUTHLAND GOLD

All Scripture quotations are taken from the King James Version of the Bible.

All of the characters and events in this book are fictitious. Any resemblance to actual persons, living or dead, or to actual events is purely coincidental.

Cover illustration by Dick Bobnick.

PRINTED IN THE U.S.A.

one

New South Wales, 1843

"Still no sign of your father, Tim?"

For a long moment there was no movement from the boy perched in the highest possible spot of the old gum tree. At last he shook his head, though continuing to stare out across the valley, searching the winding road that disappeared through the tall timber at the foot of the distant mountain. Adam knew how desperately the boy hoped to see the familiar horse and wagon carrying the man he had missed so much these last long months.

After a pause, Adam Stevens tried again. "Anything could have delayed him, Son," he called in an even louder voice. His voice was troubled, revealing his own anxiety. They had been expecting Timothy Hardy to arrive midmorning, at the latest by midday. But the sun was low in the west. Adam had been out in the back paddocks all day, and when he had returned a few moments ago, his anxious wife had met him at the homestead gate. Kate was deeply worried about Tim, who had climbed the tree hours ago and resisted all her pleas to come down.

Tim stirred slightly but never stopped watching that distant dirt track. It was a long moment before his quiet tones answered, "But Father would have allowed for that and set out even earlier than he had planned. He always camps somewhere so he can be here as early as possible. His letter said to expect him this morning. Besides, he knew I'd be waiting."

Adam's concern deepened. Tim was right. It was so unlike Timothy. After the tragedy of losing his wife and small daughter the year before, Timothy had found it especially hard to leave his beloved son at Waverley so the boy could

5

finish his schooling. More than once Adam's lonely old friend had arrived a day or so earlier than expected. And because of all that had happened, Adam had been making plans that he was eager to surprise his friend with this evening.

"Well, what if we grab a couple of horses and go meet him?" Adam forced his voice to sound cheerful.

That did bring an eager response. "Oh, Sir, could we?"

There was a rustle of leaves, and Adam watched with some relief as Tim made short work of reaching the ground. He was nowhere near as tall as Adam, but Adam knew that Tim's father would be astonished at the way the lad had grown these last few months.

"Yes, I don't see why not." He didn't give a hint how weary the hard day's work had made him, just placed his hand on the boy's shoulder and turned toward the house. "But we'd better tell Kate first. We'll get her to put together some food and water for us. If anything, we can have a picnic tea in the bush with your father," he finished with a grin.

There was no answering smile from Tim. He paced silently beside Adam for several yards before he at last took a deep breath and blurted out, "Something's happened to Father, Mr. Stevens. I–I woke up early this morning, was praying and reading the Bible like I always do, when. . ." He paused.

Adam glanced at him and noticed color creeping into his cheeks. He looked quickly away, wondering why Tim was suddenly feeling embarrassed.

The last two years, Tim had stayed with the Stevenses so he could go to the small school Kate had started years ago for the station children and any aborigines who could be persuaded to attend. During that time, they had always encouraged Tim to continue the habit of having personal devotions each morning as his father and mother had taught him. Like his parents, Tim had never been shy about his faith in God, and Adam and Kate had enjoyed many discussions with him about spiritual things.

Even when Timothy senior had been in his convict chains on board that transport ship to Australia all those years ago, he had never hesitated to talk about his Savior and Lord, Jesus Christ, no matter how many times he had suffered physical as well as verbal abuse from the other convicts. Because of his unjust treatment when trying to stop a convict riot on board ship, Timothy was granted the deeply longed for ticket of leave. Despite all the restrictions still on him until his ten years were served, that piece of paper allowed him to choose his employer and actually be paid for work. He had gladly chosen Adam as his boss.

Adam was a bitter, angry man in those days. He too had known what it was to be a convict but had met Timothy Hardy not long after becoming an emancipist, the name given to those in Australia who had finished their prison term but chosen to stay and make a new lives for themselves. Adam knew Timothy had suffered far more in his first few months than Adam had his whole term and, at the time, had marveled that the small, gentle man's attitude was so different from his own. Timothy had joined an organization in England trying to right unjust laws. Foolishly he had let himself be swept up in a riot that ended in his arrest and transportation. Despite all he had endured, Timothy's life had wonderfully demonstrated God's forgiveness, the peace and quiet joy that a personal relationship with God gave.

To his own surprise, Adam had found himself prepared to listen to Bible readings and discussions around the lonely campfires in the bush. At last he, too, had believed it was all true, accepted Christ as his own personal Savior, to find his life transformed from darkness to light. There was simply no other way to describe it all. He still often marveled in sheer wonder at his life now compared to what it had been.

Adam glanced briefly at the set face of Tim. According to Kate, the boy had seemed unusually tense all day, showing none of the excitement he usually exhibited each time his father was able to make the long journey southeast from Stevens Downs. And Tim had more reason than usual to be looking forward to his father's return. Kate had taught Tim all she could in their little school. Now he was to return home with his father for good, or at least until Kate could persuade Timothy to let them help give the bright, intelligent lad a chance at further education—perhaps in a good boarding school in Sydney. Hopefully Adam's new plans would help Timothy make those dreams possible.

Nearing the gate to the homestead, Adam asked quietly, "What happened during your devotional time, Tim?"

Tim stopped. He looked down at his boots, scuffing one of them in the dirt. Adam waited patiently until the boy at last looked up, searching Adam's face anxiously. "You'll think it's all my imagination," he said rapidly, "but I. . .it suddenly seemed as though God was telling me to pray for Father. I felt really anxious for him all of a sudden, and since then. . ."

A horse whinnied a short distance away. Tim and Adam turned as a deep, guttural voice said, "Me reckon you wantum horses like, Boss?"

Adam looked with considerable exasperation at the solemn face of a tall aborigine slouched on the back of a large black horse. Then he saw that the man was holding the reins of three other horses—two saddled and one a packhorse.

Tim gasped, and Adam said swiftly, "Jackie, how many times do I have to tell you to cut out that false native talk?"

This was an old joke between them, the European raised and educated aborigine reverting to "blackfellow" talk, especially to fool white strangers who were stupid enough to think themselves superior. But for once, there was no brief gleam of teeth as usually happened when Adam chided him. Jackie eased the wide-brimmed cattleman's hat back off his dark forehead and stared silently back.

Adam tensed, studying the expressionless face. Jackie knew something. It never ceased to amaze him how aborigines discovered things long before white people did, but Adam had learned long ago never to underestimate Jackie.

"Mr. Stevens, please, can Jackie come too?" Tim's voice held a shrill note of urgency.

Adam glanced at Tim and then back at Jackie and the horses. "Seems to me he's already decided that," he said as lightly as he could.

A faint glimmer of amusement briefly touched the black eyes. "Reckon that Missus already packum food and dem blankets for three, like," he drawled.

Adam put his hands on his hips and glared in mock anger at his old friend. "I don't know, Tim. Do you really think we should take a no-good aboriginal blackfellow along with us who tries to fool white folk with his attempts at English?"

To Adam's relief, the boy relaxed a little and a slight smile crossed his pale face.

Tim reached for the black mare that had been unofficially his ever since he had come to live with the Stevens family and patted the long nose that nudged him. "Guess you shouldn't be too hard on Jackie, Sir. After all, he has to be such a good example of an educated blackfellow when he helps Mrs. Kate at school that he probably needs a chance to be himself."

Although this was part of the same old joke between them, this time something flashed across Jackie's face. It was gone in an instant, but Adam knew that Jackie often felt the pain of being caught between two worlds. He had never been fully accepted by his own people because of his upbringing by well-meaning missionaries after the death of his mother and was rarely accepted by white people—usually only those who knew him well, loved and respected him.

Jackie straightened in his saddle. Adam wasn't in the least surprised when he said in the polished, educated accent of an upper-crust Englishman, "That is enough cheek out of you, my young man. And no more nonsense if you want to share any of this food and camping gear. Now, do you intend to stay here chatting instead of being on our way before dark?"

Only then did Adam realize the horses already had full saddlebags and blankets. He stepped forward and took his horse's reins from Jackie. "Kate?"

Jackie nodded. "I was going with a couple of the men, if

you were any later getting home."

They stared at each other in silent communication. Jackie was an excellent blacktracker. Aboriginals were noted for their ability to track animals and people over the most difficult terrain. Their feats since early settlement had never ceased to amaze the unskilled "white fellas." Now, and not for the first time by any means, Adam was glad that over the years Jackie had been sought out by police and folk from across a wide area to help find people lost in the bush or criminals seeking to escape the law.

Tension filled the air. Tim was already in his saddle. Without another word Adam mounted swiftly. Only then did he see the rifle resting in its leather holster. He always carried a revolver at his waist in case he came across badly injured stock that needed to be put down or any of a number of dangers that lurked in the bush, but if Jackie thought they might need a rifle as well, it was an ominous sign.

Kate was waiting a little wistfully for them near the gate. Adam knew that if she did not have the responsibility of their two small children, nothing would have stopped her going with them. He bent quickly for his kiss. She told him softly that she had instructed Jackie to pack enough supplies in case they had to travel all the way to Stevens Downs. Grim faced, he stared at her for a long moment.

Glancing at Tim, Kate called out an encouraging word. Then she looked back at Adam steadily. "We'll be fine here," she murmured at last, "I just hope Jackie's information is wrong. Take as long as you need, but I'll be waiting."

Adam nodded briefly, then turned his horse, and the trio set off down the stony road in a clatter of hooves. Near the gum tree he glanced back. Kate was still watching. She waved until a bend in the road took her out of sight. Adam knew she would be busy praying for them all as she waited, and especially for their old friend Timothy Hardy.

They kept the horses trotting along at a brisk pace until they reached the winding track usually taken to reach Stevens

Downs. Adam was content to let Jackie lead the way, knowing the man's sharp eyes would see any trace of a recent traveler that the other two could easily miss.

Hours later, as the brief twilight gave way to darkness, the three friends quietly set up camp on the dry creek bed at Lewis Ponds. They were sure that something had either happened to prevent Timothy Hardy from starting out or that he was sick or injured somewhere on the trail.

Jackie finished attending to the horses and then disappeared into the shadows of the bush. Adam left Tim to roll out their blankets while he started a small fire and poured some water into a blackened billy can and set it to boil.

"Sir, do you think Father could have gone the long way round on the main road from Wellington through Blackman's Swamp, even gone on to Bathurst before. . .before heading for Waverley?"

Adam's heart ached at the sound of the exhausted, trembling voice. Reluctantly he shook his head. "He could have, I guess, but he never has before—always taken you with him if he needed to go near the villages."

Low, pain-filled tones asked the inevitable question. "He. . . he still has a couple years of his sentence to go. No one would have. . .would have demanded he show them his ticket of leave, would they? And if he had lost it?"

"I'm sure that would be no problem, Tim," Adam reassured the boy. "Except for the authorities who renew his ticket each year, I doubt if many people out here even remember he was transported to Australia. He is very highly thought of in the whole district as my trusted manager of Stevens Downs." He paused and added, "I still think it's simply that he's had a horse go lame or sick on him. And you know as well as I do how well he cares for his animals."

Tim stared at Adam for a long moment. Then he looked into the deepening shadows of the surrounding bush. He knew as well as the older man the dangers in the harsh Australian bush, so different from England. During the long hours that afternoon, he had already accepted the fact that his father's plan to bring a small dray to carry home Tim's possessions would mean a much slower journey. But Tim also knew his father would have made allowance for that.

He heaved a sigh. At least his father had not intended to ride, so his horse couldn't have thrown him. But something—a snake, a startled kangaroo, any number of things—could have startled the cart horses, making them bolt. His biggest fear was that his father was lying sick or injured somewhere.

Mother had always fussed over his father whenever he had even the slightest cold. Tim knew his father's health had never been the same since his ordeal in prison and on that horrible convict ship when he had been flogged. And Tim sensed that his father hadn't fully recovered from losing Mother and Tim's three-year-old sister, Jane, from the fever last year. Tim was convinced that only faith in a God of love and mercy had kept his father sane.

During that dreadful time, Tim himself had begun to doubt that God really cared about them. All that had happened to his family these last few years would surely make anyone wonder. But he had certainly been praying today.

Tim's thoughts stayed with him throughout the evening as he sat by the campfire and then later as he struggled to fall asleep under his blanket. He also wondered where Jackie had disappeared to and why he had led them so far east of the main route to Wellington. Adam had told him that this often happened with Jackie out in the bush, but the man's absence added to Tim's unease.

The next morning, Jackie reappeared and quietly informed them that Tim's father had been last seen a long way off his usual route, near the Turon River, a few miles from where it joined the Macquarie.

Adam stared at him in the faint, predawn light. Tim knew Adam had learned a long time ago not to ask Jackie how he gained information. They had not seen a soul since they'd left Waverley, but aborigines could easily be watching them.

Tim looked from Jackie's somber face to Adam's puzzled one. "What would Father be doing over there? It's a longer way from our usual track than here at Lewis Ponds Creek."

"I don't know," Adam replied quietly. "But we had better head that way. Let's hope Jackie can find the trail there."

They made it to the Turon River and followed its winding path east through the hills and scrub until it was once again too dark to go farther in the rugged country. After another restless night on the hard ground, the silent trio set off at first light. Tim had stopped praying by then.

They found the remains of the small camp first. The dray was gone, along with the horses. Some of Timothy's meager personal belongings were scattered on the ground.

The hills rose quite steeply a little way back from the creek, and Jackie swiftly led them in that direction. When they reached an area of fallen rocks, he lost Timothy's trail.

"Spread out and walk around the edge of this," Jackie said wearily. "Keep an eye out for any tracks leading away from this stony ground."

It was Tim who found his father.

After searching the area allotted to him, he desperately plunged a little deeper into the bush and rounded a large boulder.

Tim froze. A still, slight figure lay sprawled on the ground. Rushing forward, for one horrible moment Tim thought there was no life in the still body.

"Father!" His voice was barely a harsh whisper.

Tim swallowed, tried to moisten his dry mouth, and reached out to gently touch the gray face. His heart leaped as the closed eyelashes flickered and a soft groan escaped through his father's cracked, swollen lips.

Tim grabbed his water bottle, but his shaking hand spilled the water on the still face before it splashed onto those lips. The eyelashes flickered again, and then the eyes opened. Tim's father stared into space for a brief moment before his eyelids drooped again.

"Father, oh dear Father, it's Tim. We've found you."

He suddenly remembered his companions and screamed out their names.

"Tim?" The murmur from his father was so soft, Tim barely heard it. He reached out and lovingly wiped away the water he had spilled on the dirt-streaked face. Only then did he realize the dirt was mingled with dried blood.

"Yes, it's Tim, Father," he choked out, fighting the tears that had begun to clog his throat, "and Adam and Jackie are near."

The eyes were searching, searching. His father moved his hand slightly toward him. Tim grasped it and held the callused, work-worn hand gently to his chest. His father clutched at him weakly and struggled to speak.

"Here, Father, have some water."

This time a couple mouthfuls were painfully, slowly swallowed.

"No. . .no more. Something must tell you. . .find. . .find Molly's box. . . ."

The voice was slightly stronger, but Tim still had to lean close to the barely moving lips.

"Find. . .the gold. . .love you. . .all for you. . .but. . .wrong. . . wrong. . . . God would have. . ."

The dull eyes closed once more, and the hand the boy held went slack. A sob tore from Tim. At the sound of the boy's agony, the slack hand tightened slightly.

The lips moved soundlessly. Timothy made one last effort and managed to whisper, "Jesus. . .more. . .more. . .precious than. . .gold. Jesus. . ." The wounded man fought to draw another shallow breath. His eyes looked up one last time. Tim saw them focus on him and fill with love. His father's eyes remained open, but gradually something went from them.

"Father? *Father!*"

Tim heard a rush of feet on the ground behind him, but he dared not take his eyes from his father's face. Adam bent over them, closed the empty eyes, and said in a choked voice, "I'm so sorry, Tim. Your father's gone to be with Jesus."

two

New South Wales, 1850

The wily bullock was determined to get away from the whip-cracking man on the back of the black horse. It plowed through the low scrub, twisting and turning around the scattered gum trees. The narrow creek and the steep, rock-strewn hill beyond that presented no deterrent.

Tim Hardy reluctantly hauled on the reins of his weary horse and watched the bullock disappear. It wasn't worth risking his horse's legs over one stubborn bull. Blackie didn't seem to disagree. He willingly slowed to a walk, and when the reins remained slack, stopped altogether. Once the horse's sides had stopped heaving, Blackie lowered his head to nibble at a tempting green shoot.

Frowning, Tim studied his surroundings. He had been out camping for several days with the stockmen from Waverley Station, trying to round up cattle that had strayed a long way off the property. He hadn't realized how far into the scrub he had pursued the bullock after it had broken away from the small mob of cattle. Now he wasn't quite sure where he was.

He listened intently. No sounds of men or cattle traveled on the light breeze. Even the trees around him barely rustled. A bird chirped nearby, a magpie warbled from a tall gum tree, and then a distant crow added its harsh cry to the sounds of the bush—sounds Tim had missed during those long, weary years of study in Sydney. Only a few times had he managed to sneak away from his books and lecturers to explore the bush that lined most of Port Jackson.

Tim set his horse in motion to the edge of the trickling water and paused to let Blackie have a short drink before slowly following the creek. It ran only a short distance before it flowed into a wider river that rippled over small, smooth pebbles. He frowned again as Blackie carefully picked his way along the bank. Something about this area felt familiar, but Tim very much doubted if he had come this way before—certainly not during the past year since he'd returned from Sydney and begun looking after Waverley for Adam.

The river narrowed as it curved around a pile of small boulders. The bank stood higher and the water ran faster and deeper. In the distance to the east, hills rose more steeply.

Tim hesitated. It was long after midday, and he still had to find his way back to the others. But it was more sensible to follow a river when he wasn't sure where he was. Getting lost in the Australian bush was not a pleasant experience, even though this was spring and not as hot as full summertime. Of course he knew how to survive if he were lost. His father and Adam had made sure of that.

He shrugged. It was a pleasant spot, with numerous golden wattle trees and flowering gums. Tim still had that nagging feeling he had been here before. He gave in to his curiosity and the lure of the quiet bush. Turning his horse, he tried to find an easier way along the riverbank. The farther Tim went beside the river, the more he was certain he had been here before. The hills had become steeper, but the valley had gradually widened. Several large boulders stood out among the thick scrub on the hills on the other side of the river.

Only once before, a long time ago, had he ever traveled in this direction from Waverley. He shrugged off the thought and concentrated on walking his horse safely over some particularly rough ground. A moment later he came to a place where the river was shallow once more, spreading out over a wider, flatter stretch of heavily pebbled soil. A good place to camp.

Tim froze. He had not realized how far north they had traveled. He did know this place. It was where they had found his father's wrecked campsite all those years ago.

Since those first few weeks he had refused to let the

memories of that dreadful day surface. They were too painful, too much a reminder that he was alone, despite Adam and Kate taking him into their own home and treating him like a son.

Here there was no escape.

He stared around, trying to pinpoint where he had searched, where he had so desperately run from his father's few scattered belongings.

He still had so many unanswered questions from that tragic day. Tim had desperately tried to work out what his father had been attempting to tell him. To his surprise, his mother's keepsake box had not been in its usual place at Stevens Downs. Adam had assured him that it had not been among his father's things at the campsite. Jackie had even led a group of men back to make a thorough search. They could only conclude that whoever had wrecked the camp must have stolen the box along with the dray and horses.

Adam had told Tim much later that Jackie believed Tim's father had camped beside that river before—perhaps made it a regular stop on his journeys from Stevens Downs to Waverley and back. But why? The site was far from the direct route to Wellington. What had been the attraction of this isolated place so far from even a lonely shepherd's hut? If it had not been for Jackie's blacktracking skills, they might never have found Tim's father.

What had been important enough to cause Timothy Hardy to behave so uncharacteristically?

For a long time his father's last words had haunted Tim. Were they delirious ramblings? Tim had never told anyone of his father's words about gold and Jesus. At first he had been too numb; later he had tried to forget the horrors of that dreadful day. But now, in this place, the memories would not be denied.

Tim had decided that his father's dying wish had been to impress on him how important Jesus Christ was. But then, Tim had always known the love his father had for his Lord.

Nothing had ever taken priority over that love, not even his wife and children.

Tim examined the site with adult eyes. Could his father have been trying to tell him something else as well, something about real gold?

In recent years, especially since the gold rushes in America, there had been more rumors about large deposits of gold being found in Australia. But that was all they seemed, rumors. No one had come forward to claim the reward the government was offering to anyone finding payable gold deposits.

Slowly Tim dismounted. He tethered Blackie and reluctantly made his way in the direction he had taken that day of heartbreak. He walked for several moments but paused, thinking he had heard a faint sound foreign to the call of the bush birds. He listened intently. For a moment all was still. Then he heard it again. A bright, cheery whistle.

Tim looked back. He had come quite a distance from his horse and suddenly wished he had brought his rifle with him. This area was very isolated, and over the years reports had circulated of cattle thieves and bushrangers hiding up in the hills.

Well, whoever it was seemed to have no fear of being discovered. For another moment he hesitated, then started forward as quietly as he could.

The whistle stopped abruptly, cut short in the very middle of a familiar Irish ditty.

≈

Patricia inspected the bottom of her prospector's pan closely. For one brief moment she had thought. . .

Her lips twitched in a wry grin. She had heard stories of wishful men back home in California imagining they saw the yellow color that would fulfill their dreams of wealth and glory. And a little of the real stuff would certainly finance this venture!

She shrugged and used Andy's small trowel to fill the dish with more mud and water from the riverbed. After all, there wasn't much else to do while she waited for him to return from his search for the old shepherd's hut they had been told was somewhere in this area. He seemed doubtful they had even found the right river. Certainly they had found no trace of Danny during all their travels west of Sydney.

She sighed, wondering if they would ever find him. Her lips firmed. They simply had to. So much depended on it—her father's health, their whole future.

Patricia absentmindedly swung the shallow dish, using the technique Andy had taught her on his gold claim in California last year. Always hope remained that when all the dirt was washed away a few yellow specks might settle in the bottom. At least it passed the time on a perfect day, and besides, each week they continued their search, she found herself falling more in love with this bush and its golden wattle trees and cheerful bird life.

Hopefully they would stay longer in this small valley. After that dreadful voyage across the vast Pacific Ocean, there had been all the hustle and bustle in Sydney as they got outfitted with their horses, dray, and camping gear. Neither Patricia nor Andy had realized how rough the terrain would be through the rugged Blue Mountains and the Bathurst area. It had taken them days longer to travel that far than they had expected. By then, she'd needed a good rest, as had their horses.

But at Bathurst, Patricia and Andy had heard news of a young man who fit Danny's description, so they had pushed on. Rumor had it he had been working with some shepherds on property a good distance to the northeast, near the Turon River. At the thought of the man they so desperately wanted to find, a shadow touched Patricia's heart, but she thrust it determinedly aside as she had so many times before. The bush was so peaceful and washing for gold so soothing, although it would certainly be a miracle if she found any color.

Grinning at herself, Patricia started whistling again.

She stirred the pan and then swung it carefully. Gradually the muddy water disappeared, leaving only a few small, heavier pebbles in the bottom of the dish. Something yellow flashed in the sunlight.

Patricia caught her breath. It couldn't be.

Her hands started to tremble slightly as she carefully filled the dish with water and repeated the process. There was no mistake.

Trying to dampen her rising excitement, Patricia muttered, "Of course, it's probably just what the old-timers called fool's gold." She grabbed the large bandanna in the pocket of her trousers and carefully tipped the pan's contents onto the dark material.

What if the rumors Danny had heard in the California gold fields that had sent him chasing out here to Australia were right? Perhaps it had not just been an excuse he had used to leave America. His last letter had mentioned an Australian called Hargraves who claimed that the country they were mining in California was very similar to where he had once worked in these central tablelands of New South Wales.

Feverishly, she started washing another pan of dirt. Even more gold remained from that lot.

Footsteps crunched on gravel a small distance behind her. Hurriedly, Patricia finished emptying the pan's contents onto the small pile in the bandanna and wrapped it up. Was Andy in for one big surprise!

As she straightened and started to swing around, she called out excitedly, "Andy, Danny probably is here somewhere. You'll never guess in a million years what I've—"

It wasn't Andy.

A man stood a little distance from her. His wide-brimmed hat sat low over his forehead, and she could barely see his eyes. His clothes were filthy, with several large tears on his shirt, and he looked as though shaving was not his favorite occupation. All in all he looked so tough and rough she would have never let him near the house when back home alone.

As she gaped at him, he started walking toward her.

Patricia quickly dropped the pan and thrust the bandanna into her trouser pocket. For a moment she held her ground, but the man was scowling, his face so grim she backed away a few paces. Then she paused, remembering the gun Andy had insisted she always carry in the bush. Every sense on alert, she let her hand rest on the handle of the revolver at her waist.

The man stopped also. He stared at the gun for a long moment and then glanced around briefly before his gaze came to rest on her face once more. "Sorry, I'm not Andy. Tim Hardy's the name." He paused and added slowly, "And who might you be, young man?"

Young man? Good. She managed to control her sudden grin and called back in as deep a voice as she could manage, "Howdy, Tim. The name's Pat."

He tilted his head to one side as though a little puzzled by that faint Irish lilt in her speech, but then he started toward her once more. Suddenly she panicked. Had he been watching her for long? Had he seen her excitement?

"Stay right where you are, Mister," she said as sternly as she could.

He stopped and stared, then lifted his lean brown hand to shift his hat farther back on his head. His face was as covered in dirt as the rest of him, but he was younger than she had first thought. His amber eyes glanced down once more to where her hand rested on her six-shooter. His lips twitched. "And if I don't, you're going to shoot me, right?"

She tilted up her chin. "If I need to, yes."

His lips widened, and white teeth flashed as he laughed briefly. "Not very friendly of you, Pat, my lad."

The smile transformed his face, and something in Patricia eased a little.

Not moving his gaze from hers, he started forward slowly. She stood her ground. His lips straightened, but as he came closer she could see amusement still sparkling in those light brown eyes. She began to back away, but anger started to rise over any fear. He was treating her like a naughty child.

Patricia stopped dead and reached for her gun. Pointing it steadily at him, she said firmly, "Not another step, Tim."

He did stop at that. All trace of amusement was wiped from his face. "Didn't your parents ever teach you it's extremely rude to point guns at strangers with no provocation?" he snapped.

"On the contrary, Pa made sure I knew how to defend myself almost as soon as I could walk," she retorted.

"A shame he didn't teach you some manners as well," he shot at her angrily. "What are you doing here?"

"None of your business."

He glared at her and then searched the area once more as if to see if she were alone. His gaze settled on the low cliff a little distance away. Sudden emotion she could not understand flared across his face. Beneath his dark tan, his face lost color. His lips tightened to a thin line.

Slowly Tim's gaze returned to her face. She thought she caught a glimpse of pain and grief in his eyes before they swiftly filled with suspicion and anger. He suddenly seemed more worn, much older.

"Anything that happens in this particular spot is very much my business," he said harshly. "Where's your camp?"

She remained silent, puzzled at the sudden change from friendly to hostile. But then, not many people enjoyed being held off at the point of a gun.

He took an angry stride closer, and she froze. "I'll. . .I'll shoot you if I have to!"

Her voice had risen, and she despised the tremble in it. To her relief, he paused. For a brief moment Patricia thought the expression in his eyes softened slightly as he studied her.

He suddenly looked behind her. "Okay, Mate, you can grab him now."

Patricia swung around. As she realized she had been fooled by one of the oldest tricks, Tim's hand grabbed the wrist of her hand that held the gun. In the same movement his other arm looped around her waist and flung her down to the ground. He banged her hand against a rock. The pain made her scream. Instead of releasing its hold, her finger tightened on the trigger. The crack of the gun made her go still.

Tim roared with pain.

Patricia dropped the revolver, crying out, "Oh no, oh no, don't tell me I've killed him."

An astonished voice cried out near her ear. "You've shot me!"

"I'm. . .oh dear, I'm so sorry."

"You'd better be!" he roared.

He didn't need to keep such a strong grip on her wrists or hold her down with his body as he squirmed to look at the damage. Fright kept her motionless. What would he do in retaliation?

Silence hung in the air.

"Lucky for you, young man, I think it's just a flesh wound."

Young man? He still thought. . .

Her first reaction was relief. But he was still sprawled all over her, and there had been just enough amusement in the cool tones to infuriate her. She gave a huge heave and managed to partly dislodge him. Her fist connected with his face even as his hands grabbed at her shirt. The top buttons went flying.

He gasped. Horror filled his face. "What the—"

A loud crack rang in their ears. A bullet hit the ground near them.

They both froze.

"Reckon you'd better get away from her if you don't want the next bullet in your hide," Andy's voice yelled furiously from behind them.

three

Without moving off the lithe body pressed into the ground under him, Tim swung his head around. A tall man was rushing down the riverbank. The stranger held two revolvers that were aimed right at Tim.

This could not be happening. In a daze, Tim stared back at the unmistakable feminine curves under him. Two green eyes sparked fury and embarrassment at him. Heat flooded his face, and he snatched his hands from her softness.

Not fast enough for the gunman.

Something cold pressed hard against Tim's back, and the man roared, "Get off her! Now! And get those hands in the air where I can see them. Move!"

The body under Tim tried to heave him off. The gun barrel eased only slightly from his spine.

Tim moved.

"You all right, Girl?"

Gimlet green eyes never left Tim as he scrambled to his feet. Pain knifed through his leg. Some stubborn, indignant streak he hadn't realized he possessed made him bite back a groan of pain and keep his hands lowered but well in sight.

"Of course I'm all right," the "girl" snapped breathlessly.

Tim could not keep himself from turning his head from the two guns trained on him and watching her scramble to her feet. She clutched the shirt across her chest. Her face remained almost as red as her fiery hair. The wide-brimmed hat had fallen off, and it seemed that her head of curls danced gold in the sunlight.

Now that he wasn't concentrating on a gun in her hand, Tim wondered how he could ever have mistaken her beautiful face for that of a boy. As she fumbled to close up her

24

shirt, he opened his mouth to apologize, but that stubborn
streak made him snap it shut and glare from her back to the
gray-haired man still staring at him with narrowed, danger-
ous eyes set in a weathered face. If anyone should apologize,
it wasn't Tim Hardy!

"Oh, Andy! Put those guns away. Can't you see he's unarmed? It was my gun that went off. Sometimes I think you
must want to be back in Nevada with your gunslinger friends."

Tim's eyes widened. Nevada? Wasn't that somewhere in
America? But their accents sounded more like the old Irishman who worked at Waverley.

The black holes of the two gun barrels did not waver.

Tim remained stubbornly silent. He looked back at the girl—
no, woman would be more accurate. The color had left her
face, leaving it pale and strained. She was holding the hand he
had slammed onto the ground. Regret swept through him. He
had been taught to be gentle, to care for women, but he had not
been gentle with her.

Tim gritted his teeth and managed to say calmly, "Pity you
hadn't realized I was unarmed, *Pat,* before you drew your gun
on me."

Patricia stared at the young man, still feeling dazed that her
gun had actually gone off. "Well. . .I. . .you startled me. I
thought. . ." Andy flashed a look at her, and she stopped. She
would never hear the end of this from him.

"What happened?" her uncle asked, still in that hard, cold
voice that chilled her. His eyes were fixed on the young man
as he added, "And it had better be a good answer."

"To start with, I didn't know the person who pulled a gun
on me for no reason whatsoever was a. . .a *woman!*"

Patricia tilted her chin but avoided Tim's accusing glare.
She swallowed a couple times before at last muttering, "He. . .
he came out of nowhere. I heard footsteps and thought it was
you. He startled me and. . .and I didn't want him too close."
She didn't think it wise to mention the yellow grains that had
so absorbed her attention she had not realized anyone had

been approaching. "Oh, do put those guns away, Andy," she added impatiently.

The guns barrels lowered slightly. Her uncle was still scowling. He didn't take his eyes from Tim as he said, "And so you tried to hold him off with your gun. I heard it go off. Did he attack you?"

"No, I didn't attack him—her," Tim yelled, "at least not until she pulled that stupid gun. For some strange reason, I just don't like a gun pointed at me for *no* reason."

Patricia noticed Andy's lips twitch slightly, and she relaxed a little. But the faint trace of amusement seemed to infuriate Tim.

He roared, "The gun went off when I tried to make her drop it. I thought he—she—was about to attack me. I swear I didn't know she wasn't a boy until I felt. . .saw. . ."

It was not a wise reminder. Andy stiffened. The guns leveled once more.

Patricia didn't blame Tim for stopping abruptly. Andy was even scaring her. Only once before had she seen that expression on his face. That horrible day before he had gone out to find the Indian who had killed her mother.

She swung her gaze back to the furious young man. Heat rose in her face again. Never before had anyone touched her so intimately. What her uncle must have thought!

After a long pause, Tim added in a quieter, puzzled voice, "It's you two who are in the middle of nowhere. What are you doing way out here? It sounds as though you're a long way from home."

He looked around, searching the immediate area. Once more he stared for a long moment at some point beyond Patricia. Momentarily his expression changed, but before she could understand the expression on his face, it disappeared. He looked back at her and asked harshly, "Are you camped nearby?"

Patricia studied him and then looked at Andy. He was still watching Tim closely, but he glanced briefly at her and slowly lowered the revolvers to his side. To her considerable relief, he expertly slipped them back into the holsters low on his hips.

Very expertly. Patricia frowned.

From the moment just before they'd boarded the ship in California until that night after they'd left Sydney, Andy hadn't worn his guns. In the past she had often teased him that they made him look like a gunfighter. He had always replied with some joking comment, but now she wondered.

She had never actually seen Andy draw them before, nor had she seen him so riled, so hard and cold, except that horrible time after her mother. . . She slammed the thought shut once more. Not for the first time, she wondered about Andy's years as a cowboy in the plains of America before he settled on land in California with her mother and father. He seldom talked about his past. Perhaps he had really been a gunfighter after all.

"We might ask you the same thing." Andy's voice brought her attention back to the current situation. "What's your name?"

Tim stared at the older man. "I'm Tim Hardy from Waverley Station," he answered curtly. Noting their blank looks, he added tersely, "It's a cattle and sheep property a few days' ride from here toward Bathurst. We've been rounding up stray cattle."

"We?" drawled the man the girl had called Andy.

Tim's leg had started to burn fiercely. "Me and three of our station hands," he snapped as he tried to ease his weight onto his good leg.

"You're bleeding!"

At the girl's dismayed cry, Tim looked down and saw that a dark stain had seeped through his trouser leg. As he moved, the wound stung, and he felt a warm trickle slide down his leg.

"Guess that's what happens when guns go off," he muttered angrily and glared at her. The pain stabbed him, and he swayed as he tried to balance on one leg.

The girl went white.

A strong hand grabbed his elbow, and Andy said with a slight

Irish lilt, "Reckon you'd better sit down before you keel over." When Tim had been eased down to the ground, Andy added tersely, "Can't be too bad or there'd be a lot more blood."

Tim thought there seemed to be more than enough blood trickling down into his boot. He concentrated on not letting them see just how painful it was. He failed miserably when Andy touched his leg. A groan ripped from him, and Tim shut his eyes. But Andy paused and was a little more gentle as he briefly examined the wound.

"Yeah, reckon you're lucky," Andy concluded. "Looks like it's just a flesh wound."

Lucky? Tim snorted and opened his eyes to look straight into brilliant green ones filled with tears of remorse.

"I'm really, really sorry," she whispered.

Tim was struck dumb. *She has the most beautiful eyes I've ever seen.*

"You got your horse hereabouts?" Andy's sharp voice was an intrusion.

Tim blinked and looked away, straight into another set of green eyes. These were much paler, knowing. They narrowed and held a hint of temper as Andy glanced from Tim to the girl and back again.

It took Tim a moment to remember the question. "Quite some distance downstream," he muttered hoarsely.

Andy dragged out a large piece of rag and started to wrap it tightly around the wound that was dripping blood onto the ground. Tim shuddered and not simply from the increased pain. He had been taught to be very careful to put only clean linen on open wounds. But dirty or not, at least the rag might control the bleeding.

Andy frowned at his makeshift bandage. "Our camp and horses are upstream."

"I didn't hear you come past here on your way back to camp. Did you find—" The girl's slightly surprised voice stopped abruptly.

Tim glanced up from examining his leg and saw the warning look the man was giving her.

Andy scowled when he saw Tim staring at him and said briskly, "You may only have a flesh wound, but it's deep, and it's still bleeding too much for you to try and walk that far." He glanced around, squinted at the sun low in the west, and heaved an annoyed sigh. "We'd best be moving our camp here for the—"

"No!"

Andy stared. He raised an eyebrow, and Tim realized how panicked he must have sounded. Swiftly he added, "I can't stay here. It. . .it's. . ." He hesitated and looked over toward the place he knew would haunt him until he died.

"There's bad memories here for me," Tim muttered at last and glanced at the girl.

She was watching him curiously. Andy snorted angrily. To Tim's immense relief, the girl said swiftly, "But we have our tent up and everything set out, Andy. And what about his horse? One of us will have to fetch it. Would not it be much easier and faster for you to go and bring his horse back here while I wait with Mr. Hardy?"

"And that would be the stupidest thing I've heard you say yet," Andy exploded. "You felt threatened enough to pull a gun on him, and now you want me to leave you here alone with him?"

"And haven't we just decided my pulling a gun was unnecessary?" she retorted.

Her hands settled on her hips, and she and her uncle glared at each other. Tim couldn't help admiring the sparks that flashed between the two.

"Besides," she added stubbornly, "I can hold my gun on him again if he tries anything."

"He'd better not try anything!" Andy roared.

Tim saw the threatening scowl leveled at him and knew that the man's roar was more for his benefit than the girl's.

"Unlike some people, I'm not stupid," Tim retorted sharply. "I'm already feeling what she can do when she's being stupid."

Andy glared at him, then looked at the defiant girl. Color rose in her pale cheeks, but she glared right back. He shrugged and then studied Tim again.

Unexpectedly Andy grinned, his eyes lighting up in sardonic amusement. "Well, if you think you'll be safe with her, guess I'll leave you two youngens to be stupid together."

Tim opened his mouth and snapped it shut, staring after Andy as he loped swiftly away toward the bush lining the river. In a few moments the older man had disappeared from sight.

Upstream they would have to go right past where Father died.

Tim closed his eyes tightly.

The journey back to Waverley that dreadful day had passed in a daze, but he remembered Jackie quietly telling him all the signs showed that his father had tumbled down the rocks a few days before. Why his father had been in this isolated place or why he had risked climbing up that cliff had never been discovered. They had only been able to speculate that he might have been hiding from whomever had wrecked his camp.

The old familiar ache settled in Tim's heart. He tore his gaze away. The young woman was still watching him curiously.

"Why do you keep looking up there? Is that where something bad happened?"

He swallowed hard and nodded briefly. He averted his eyes, looking down at his leg. Blood had already started to seep through the rag.

"Whatever did I do to make you feel so threatened you drew your gun on me?" Tim asked, hoping she would not ask him any more questions. Although many questions had hovered in his mind about that black day, he had never been able to talk about it again, not even to Adam or Kate.

A shrewd look crossed the girl's face as she surveyed him. He moved restlessly. Something in the way she stared at him told him she'd guessed he didn't want to talk about the "bad" thing that had happened. A flash of sympathy touched her eyes, and she looked swiftly away, but not before he had seen her lips tighten, the pain that filled her face. She obviously had her own bad memories, understood about experiences too painful to talk about.

She stared for a long moment toward the place near the water where he had first seen her. A large tin plate of some kind rested on the ground as if she had dropped it when he had startled her. She must have been washing it or something. After a moment she glanced back at him, and Tim was surprised at the apprehension on her face before she looked back at the creek.

The silence lengthened. Her hands clenched into fists, and she stood so tensely that Tim felt his anger start to rise once more. No one had ever been afraid of him. He cleared his throat. "Would you consider me too threatening if I asked your name and what you are doing here?"

She jumped slightly at his loud, sarcastic voice and swung around. A strange expression filled her face as though her mind had been on something completely different. Then a look of apprehension returned. She bit her lip and crossed her arms in front of her, hugging herself as though she were getting cold.

"I'm. . .I'm sorry." She swallowed and added with an attempt at a smile, "I'm being very bad mannered, aren't I?"

"Bad mannered?" he exploded. "I would hope your parents would have clipped you in the ear for having such bad manners you'd aim a gun at a man for no reason!"

Her expression changed in a flash. All remorse gone, she glared back at him and opened her mouth, thought better of whatever she was going to say, and swallowed instead. "Yes, Pa would certainly have done just that," she muttered and then blurted out, "You. . .you are so pale. Your leg must be very painful."

He stared at her silently and waited.

"Patricia Casey," she said, abruptly answering his question. "And my uncle is Andy O'Donnell. We were hoping to. . .to meet up with. . ." She hesitated and then added, "With an old friend out this way, but I guess it's unlikely he's here."

Tim raised his eyebrows. "Very unlikely. As far as I know even the nearest shepherd's hut is many miles from here."

Excitement flashed into those incredible eyes. "So there is a hut somewhere in this area," he thought he heard her murmur. He moved his leg slightly, and the pain made him grit his teeth.

After a deep breath, he said irritably, "Afraid I can't say it's been a pleasure to meet you, Patricia Casey."

Color swept into her face, and she bit her lip. She swung away, and he watched her long, angry strides as she went over and picked up the dish near the water's edge. As she straightened, she looked beyond him toward the trees and froze.

He glanced swiftly around but saw nothing. When he looked back at Patricia, she was racing toward him, her hand grabbing for that gun of hers once more.

"Natives," she gasped. "There. Two of them."

Tim looked swiftly in the direction of her pointing finger. In the dark shadows of the bush, two aborigines stood staring at them, as still as statues. Both were naked except for their loincloths. Both were carrying several long spears. Even more menacing was the way their bodies were painted with white clay and yellow ochre.

Ignoring the pain, Tim scrambled awkwardly to his feet. The two aborigines moved slowly out into the sunlight, and he sighed with relief. One of them was Jackie. So that was why Jackie had refused to go on the muster to help find the strays—aboriginal business.

Tim looked at Patricia to tell her, then paused. Once again she had whipped out that wretched gun. His gaze narrowed. If ever anyone needed to be taught a lesson. . .

Making a split decision, he ordered in a low voice, "Put that gun away."

She glance at him indecisively.

"Now!"

To his relief, she obeyed him. On the whole, there had not been strife between whites and blacks for some years in the Bathurst and Orange areas. But in the past, the military had been called out too many times to "teach the natives a lesson" using guns and death, so even Jackie would not be complacent about a gun being pointed at him.

Tim called out loudly, *"Wanjibaayn waajin."*

To his relief, Jackie paused and studied Patricia. He must have decided that she was indeed the "naughty white woman" Tim had called out. He said something to his companion and after a moment yelled back in rapid Wiradjuri.

Over the years Tim had learned much of the local aboriginal language from Jackie, but he understood it only if it was spoken slowly and clearly—something Jackie knew well. By speaking so quickly, Jackie was letting Tim know he, too, could play games. Tim had understood only two words that Jackie had spoken. *"Guuwiyn"* meant "white man," and *"yaambul"* meant "nonsense or a lie."

Jackie's voice sounded threatening, and to Tim's dismay, Patricia once more held that gun. Hoping Jackie was close enough to hear, Tim said loudly, "Put your gun away, Patricia. They feel threatened."

She looked at him from wide, frightened eyes. "The. . .the savages back home paint themselves when they are on raiding parties," she gasped.

He relented. She was really scared. "They won't hurt us," he said swiftly. "They look like they are just passing through to a corroboree somewhere."

"Co. . .corrob. . . ?"

"A kind of native dance."

Jackie called out again, this time more slowly. Tim heard real anxiety in the man's voice as Jackie asked if Tim was all right or needed help. He must have noticed the rag on Tim's leg.

Tim relented, suddenly feeling foolish. "I'm okay, Jackie," he called back in English.

Jackie hesitated and then waved the handful of spears in his hand. The next moment both men had disappeared as quietly as they had come.

"They. . .they've gone," Patricia gasped. "Do you think they will come back when it gets dark?"

She was trembling badly. Tim regretted his impulse to punish her. "No, they won't be back," he assured her swiftly. "One of them works for us." He didn't think it necessary to tell her that he was almost certain the other aborigine was Mirrang, who had also worked at Waverley periodically over the years.

Those glorious eyes searched the bush and then turned on him. "You called him Jackie."

Feeling guilty, Tim nodded briefly and looked away.

She did not move. Tim risked a quick glance at her. To his relief, her color was slowly returning. She started putting her gun away, and he was relieved to see she had stopping shaking. He had probably been rather foolish to upset her when she had her finger on that trigger.

"And how well do you know this Jackie, I wonder?" she murmured. Suspicion had crept into her eyes. "I don't suppose by any chance you were trying to frighten me out of my wits?"

Respect filled him. She was so different from most of the girls who had tried to befriend him when he had been at college in Sydney. This was one very intelligent woman.

"Rather *stupid* of me." He could not stop the grin that twitched at his lips.

Temper flared for a moment in her face. "Guess you don't know my mother was killed by an Indian."

He was stunned to silence. No wonder she had reacted the way she had! "I'm sorry," he at last muttered weakly.

Patricia looked away. "A. . .a small number of Indians raided our first ranch." He saw her swallow several times, then draw a deep breath before adding softly, "It was a long time ago."

So she did have bad memories.

While Tim was trying to find the right words to say, she

suddenly straightened her shoulders, looked back at him, and said steadily, "Guess this means we are even."

"Guess it does," he said seriously.

They stood eyeing each other in awkward silence. Then Tim imagined what Jackie must be thinking right now. His lips twitched and a soft chuckle burst from him. At the return of her frown, he said hurriedly, "I'm sure your Andy would agree."

Relief swept through him when a reluctant smile chased away her anger. "Well," she whispered conspiratorially, "let's not tell him."

They grinned at each other, then started to chuckle. The chuckles became roars of laughter until Tim moved his leg unwarily and his laugh turned to a groan. Carefully he slid back down to the ground.

The light died out of her face, and she sat down beside him. "But at least I didn't get a spear in my leg." Her face was full of regret. "I really am so sorry about hurting you."

He couldn't bear to see a shimmer of tears in those beautiful eyes that had so recently been lit with laughter. "There was never a moment's danger of that," he reassured her quickly. "I've known Jackie since I was a boy."

She was silent for a moment. "And I don't suppose he taught you to speak his language by any chance?" she asked mildly. "And you haven't taught him English by any chance?"

"Er, yes, he did teach me," Tim answered sheepishly, deciding to be honest with her. "But I didn't have to teach him English. He was adopted by white missionaries after his father disappeared and his mother died."

Patricia stared at him and then sprang to her feet, avoiding his gaze.

"I. . .I didn't understand more than a couple of words he said that first time," Tim rushed to say, hoping she would not retreat again. "But I think he either called me a nonsense white man or a lying one."

She muttered something that sounded like, "Both would be

appropriate."

Regret swept through him. His mother and father would be so disappointed in him for being called a liar. "God hates liars," they had often told him.

Patricia picked up the dish she had dropped when she saw the aborigines. Without looking at Tim, she turned away, tossing over her shoulder, "I'm going for a walk. Perhaps I'll meet Andy coming back."

Tim opened his mouth to protest as she headed downstream and then snapped it closed. In a moment she had disappeared around an old gum tree that had fallen down the bank during some distant flood when this small trickle of water had been transformed into a swirling river of mud and debris.

The silence of the bush settled around Tim. He raised his eyes and looked toward the spot where he had held his dying father so long ago.

"Well, Father, I never thought I would be able to laugh here of all places," he murmured.

Suddenly he realized that the devastating anguish he used to feel when he thought of those last moments with his father was gone. Perhaps he should have had the courage to return here years ago as Adam and Kate had gently suggested.

A loud scream rang out. A woman's scream.

Patricia.

Ignoring the pain, Tim scrambled to his feet as fast as he could. As he started forward, she scrambled over the fallen tree and rushed toward him.

"Ab. . .abo. . .aborigines," she panted frantically. "They've got Andy!"

four

For a moment Tim stopped dead. There had been no serious trouble with the aborigines in the area for a long time. But there was always the chance. . . .

He'd thought Jackie had been going to some tribal ceremony, one of their dances, an initiation, perhaps something as simple as a ceremonial hunting party. But an aborigine raised by white people and eager for acceptance by his own people might agree to anything to achieve that. And if it were some special gathering of the tribes that Jackie was on his way to, there would be other aborigines from near and far to impress.

"Get those filthy spears away from me." Andy's roar carried clearly to both Tim and Patricia. "Give me back my guns you. . .you limbs of Satan!"

Tim tried to hurry toward the source of the ruckus. Patricia had caught up with him, and he heard her gasp of horror as a strange procession came into sight. Two aborigines were herding Andy before them. To Tim's dismay, neither was Jackie. As Andy tried to turn around, one of them prodded him with a long spear. Andy roared again.

Another aborigine appeared. He was riding Blackie.

Tim breathed a sigh of relief as he recognized Jackie. Using his native tongue, the aborigine yelled out to Tim. Although the words came too fast for Tim to understand clearly, he knew Jackie was concerned that Andy was trying to steal Tim's horse.

"Jackie," Tim yelled back, "let him go! He isn't a horse thief. He was just getting Blackie for me because I've injured my leg."

Both natives with Andy stilled. They looked at each other and then at their captive. Tim breathed easier. Obviously they also understood what he had said. They lowered their spears, and Andy stumbled away from them toward Tim.

He stuttered in his fury. "You. . .you. . .these are friends of yours?"

Tim nodded helplessly and continued to limp slowly forward.

Andy roared again and advanced on him. "I should have shot you myself. You—" Speechless in his fury, he shook his fist at Tim as the distance between them narrowed.

One of Jackie's companions, who Tim now recognized as Mirrang, raised the spear in his hand menacingly.

Patricia cried out.

Tim stopped dead. Not taking his eyes from the raised spear, he said sharply, "Andy, don't move." Then he yelled out, *"Mirrang, marrambang!"*

Mirrang didn't move.

Andy stopped and swung toward the aborigine. When he saw the spear posed to throw, he froze. A breath of relief hissed through Tim's teeth.

Still Mirrang did not move.

Had he used the right word for "friend"? Tim's concern deepened. He didn't know the older aborigine very well, although Mirrang had worked on Waverley some years ago for Elizabeth Waverley, the woman who was married to John Martin and had sold the station to Adam and Kate.

"Jackie, please tell Mirrang that Andy's a friend."

Tim saw Jackie's lips move. Mirrang ignored him. Jackie spoke more sharply, and to Tim's immense relief, Mirrang slowly lowered the threatening spear.

No one moved.

"Jackie, give the white fella back his guns and let him have my horse."

Jackie stared at Tim and then took his time studying first Andy and then Patricia.

Tim waited. He had learned a long time ago to wait for Jackie.

"Reckon you one crazy boss-man," Jackie said at last in heavily accented English, a sign of how angry and disgusted he was.

Jackie dropped Blackie's reins, turned, and strode away. Realizing that Jackie had not given him his familiar salute with the spears, Tim did not look forward to the next time they met.

Mirrang stared from one white person to the next. He angrily shook his handful of spears and followed Jackie and the other aborigine into the bush.

Blackie tossed his head and turned to follow Jackie. Tim let out a piercing whistle and the horse swung round, tossing his head up and down. At Tim's second whistle, the horse started ambling toward him. Andy moved swiftly and grabbed Blackie's bridle. Tim was relieved to see the gun belt slung across the saddle.

A slight figure flew past Tim. Patricia flung herself into Andy's arms. "Andy, Andy, are you all right? I was so frightened."

The horse snorted and pulled back on its reins. Andy held them tightly but wrapped an arm around the shaking girl. "Easy there, Girl, of course I am. They crept up on me, jabbed me with their spears when I was busy trying to get the horse, but I doubt there's more than a scratch or so."

Tim reached them and started soothing Blackie. He felt absolutely wretched. If he had not started that nonsense with Jackie, Patricia would not be so shaken and pale, so different from the courageous young woman who had not hesitated to pull a gun on him.

"Oh, Andy, if anything had happened to you, how would I find Danny all by myself in this dreadful country?"

Andy glanced sharply at Tim. He murmured something to his niece. She let him go and looked at Tim. He kept rubbing Blackie's neck, pretending he had not noticed. Whatever their business with this Danny, it was not his concern. Shame swept through him. He wanted nothing more than to get up on Blackie and leave, but the pain in his leg was considerably worse. He suspected the wound had started to bleed more since he had put weight on it.

Reluctantly Tim called out, "Mr. O'Donnell, I'm afraid I'm going to need your help getting up in the saddle. The sooner I can get this leg tended to, the better."

Andy took his time strapping his gun belt to his waist before marching up to Tim. "And I'm thinking that once you're on that horse, you'd best be on your way and about your own business, Mister. We've had enough trouble for one day."

Before Tim could reply, Patricia cried out, "But he's injured. We have to—"

"We don't have to do anything, Pat," her uncle replied sternly, "and we don't owe him anything. If he hadn't jumped you, his leg wouldn't have stopped that bullet."

"But I pulled a gun on him first," she pleaded. "You've already said we were both at fault. It will be dark soon, and his men will be too far away for him to reach. Besides," she added swiftly, "he did rescue you from those aborigines. What if they come back?"

Tim stared at Patricia in astonishment. He had frightened her so badly that she had pulled a gun on him. He'd jumped on her, hurt her hand, and allowed her to be scared to death. And after all that, she was pleading for him? What sort of woman was this?

A woman just like Mother.

The thought slammed into him. His father had once laughingly told Tim to make sure he found a wife "just like your mother." Mollie Hardy had blushed and scolded her husband, but Tim had never forgotten. He had adored his mother. She had been a woman with a great sense of humor, an immense capacity to love, and an even greater faith in God. His mother had loved her husband and children fiercely, joyfully caring for them in the very best way she could.

It had taken great courage and love for her to forgive her

husband for letting himself become embroiled in political unrest the way he had. When he had been arrested with other rioters, she had fought for him. When that had failed to stop his transportation to Australia, without hesitation she had packed Tim's and her own bags and followed her husband across those fifteen thousand miles of ocean from England. It had been Elizabeth Waverley, a passenger who had befriended Timothy on board ship, who had paid their fare.

And now Patricia—this courageous, compassionate young woman who shared his own sense of the ridiculous—reminded Tim of that mother.

Andy O'Donnell was still hesitating as Patricia pleaded, "I'm sure he'd be able to tell us the best and easiest way to get to Wellington, or Orange even, from here. At least let us attend to his wound properly first."

Andy just stared at her. Patricia wasn't quite sure just why she was so anxious to help Tim Hardy. Certainly she had an obligation to make sure the wound she had inflicted was cared for, but something else had happened to her when they had laughed together. She had felt that she'd found a friend. And friends had been very scarce in recent years.

Their ranch had been primitive and isolated. Danny and her mother had always been her best friends. After Patricia's mother had been killed, her father had changed radically, becoming harsh and unreasonable. Her brother had finally given up trying to work with him, packed his bags, and gone to join the army and fight the war with Mexico. The day the news had reached them that he had been reported missing and was believed killed, her father had changed even more, blaming himself bitterly for the deaths of both his wife and his only son.

And then last year. . . Patricia shuddered and tried to push aside the memories. The joy. The pain. The California gold rush had been the last straw. It had turned her world upside down.

Patricia pushed away those memories and watched Tim calm

his horse. Here was someone who shared her sense of humor, someone like herself who had not thought twice about tackling a person holding a gun on him. This last year she had met so many men with bold glances who had made her cringe and be very wary of her femininity. His embarrassment and confusion when he had realized she wasn't a young man had touched something deep inside her. But what really intrigued her about Tim Hardy were the flashes of sadness that occasionally darkened his strong face, making him look so vulnerable.

Tim looked at her uncle. "If you give me a leg up, I'll be on my way." His chin was set at a stubborn angle that matched his brisk words.

Patricia looked pleadingly at Andy.

He stared at her with his hands on his hips, gave a snort, and stepped forward. "Hold the horse, Pat, while I heave this bloke up."

When she did not move, he sighed and said, "All right. We'll let him camp with us tonight, and we'll see what happens tomorrow."

She smiled at Andy affectionately before moving to help. Her uncle presented a tough image to the world, but she knew what a compassionate man he could be to those he cared about.

Tim was gray and perspiration beaded his forehead by the time he swung up onto the saddle. As they started off, Patricia saw him grit his teeth when Blackie scrambled up the low bank. She watched him carefully, but he kept his head down as they followed the river upstream.

When they passed the place Tim had seemed disturbed by, Patricia looked around, searching the area for some clue as to why it affected him. Then, near the slope of stones and dirt that looked as though it must have slid down the hillside some time ago, she saw something on a large old gum tree that made her catch her breath.

She glanced at the two men. Tim still had his head down. Andy was as close to him and the horse as the narrow track

would permit. As she opened her mouth to draw their attention to the roughly constructed cross, Tim swayed in the saddle, and Andy reached up to steady him.

She quickened her own pace. Time enough to mention what
she had seen when Tim had been attended to. No doubt he
already knew what was there in any event, and that's why he
kept his head down. Her heart went out to him in understanding. Some dreadful tragedy had happened in this place, and
Tim still carried its mark.

When they stopped at their camp, Tim swayed forward
onto the horse's neck. The black horse moved restlessly.
Patricia called out and rushed forward. Andy was already
reaching for him.

Tim gasped, "Sorry. . .feel sick."

Although Tim was not a particularly tall man, his size was
such that both Patricia and Andy were panting by the time
they had eased him from the saddle and half-carried him to
their tent.

Dazed eyes gazed briefly up at them from his pale face.
"Sorry," he gasped before his head fell back and he passed out.

Patricia gave a little distressed cry, but Andy murmured
compassionately, "Ah, the poor lad. Just as well he's out of it
while we get this boot off and. . ." He paused and added a little
more urgently, "No wonder he's fainted. This is full of blood.
Silly young fool—brave but foolish."

He glanced up at his niece and frowned at her. "Now, now,
no more tears, Pat, me dear. From what you've both said, the
gun went off accidentally. Get some fresh water while I get
this boot off. We'll hopefully have this cleaned up properly by
the time he comes to."

They almost succeeded in doing just that. Tim stirred as
Patricia finished wrapping his freshly dressed leg in the piece
of clean linen ripped from the only petticoat she had in her
kit. She had been shocked at just how bad the wound was.

As Tim groaned and tried to sit up, Andy said softly,
"Quiet, Boy, we are almost finished. I'm afraid you've lost

quite a bit of blood. You can have some water in a moment. We'll have a fire going in no time and get some food into you too. Hopefully you'll be feeling much better soon."

Although Tim managed to drink some tea made in the blackened can, he ate very little. At first Tim refused, but eventually Andy managed to persuade him to drink some rum. "We brought it for medicinal purposes," the older man insisted. "Afraid it's all we've got to take the edge off your pain and help you get some sleep, Son. We used some to wash out the wound, but it will probably do more good inside you."

Tim stared from Andy to Patricia and muttered something that sounded like, "Hope you aren't watching, Mother." Then he spluttered and choked as he downed the fiery spirits. Whether it was from the rum or from sheer exhaustion, he finally fell asleep, much to Patricia's relief.

Andy chuckled. "Not often you meet a young man who is not at all used to alcohol," he mused.

"Danny wasn't before. . ." She bit her lip.

Andy finished her thought gently. "A lot of things didn't happen before your dear mother, my sister, died." He sighed and added bracingly, "We had better get something to eat ourselves. If I'm not mistaken, we may be in for a restless night with this lad."

Unfortunately he was right. Tim tossed and turned most of the night, giving them little rest. Although the bleeding seemed to have stopped, by morning his cheeks were a little flushed.

"We've got to get you to your home for proper medical care," Patricia said firmly after very carefully bathing and redressing the red-looking wound.

"Home," he muttered. A strange look filled his eyes. Pain. A great loneliness. Then he scowled and closed his eyes once more.

When Tim didn't move for several minutes, Patricia reluctantly left him to find Andy. He shook his head over the idea of leaving. "I suppose we could try him lying down in the dray, but you know how rough it was getting here through the scrub. It's probably a long way to his place, and he has lost too much blood to risk starting up the bleeding all over again from the jolting he'd get."

"But he needs a doctor!"

Andy grimaced. "Wouldn't be the first bullet wound I've doctored, me darlin'."

With that, she had to be content.

As the morning wore on, Tim became pale, losing the flush in his cheeks. Although Patricia and Andy knew he was still in pain, Tim point-blank refused to drink anymore rum, and they were both immensely relieved when at last he dozed off.

Andy stared down at Tim's still body for a long moment before moving away. He tilted his wide-brimmed hat onto the back of his head. "Might as well not waste time here. It's almost midday, but think I'll head downstream and see if there's any trace of that shepherd or his hut. Might be a track leading from the creek."

He looked at Patricia's doubtful face and added abruptly, "That man in Bathurst seemed quite definite that someone answering Danny's description went to this region with the old shepherd. I'll take the black horse. Ours was limping a little yesterday and should be rested."

Patricia hesitated, glancing uncertainly toward Tim.

"Reckon he owes us that much," Andy drawled.

The young man's horse was certainly younger and fitter than the saddle horse they had purchased in Sydney. Andy's chin was set at the angle Patricia recognized from of old. She shrugged, knowing he had hated riding their sluggish old horse and would never listen to her protests about needing to ask permission.

When Andy tried to mount Blackie, the horse objected strongly, but Andy was a skilled horseman and swiftly brought the snorting horse under control before riding off.

"What's he doing with Blackie?"

Patricia spun around. Tim was at the entrance of the tent.

Even as she rushed to prevent him from taking another step, he sat down in the dirt with a groan.

"You mustn't move! You might start the bleeding—Oh dear. You have already."

Tim resisted her efforts to make him go back to his makeshift bed, so she fussed over him, dragging the folded blankets under his leg to keep it elevated as Andy had shown her. To her dismay, Tim's cheeks were flushed once more. She touched his forehead with the back of her hand. "Now you have the beginnings of a fever. Please do lie still. Andy's only gone to try and find someone we were told was around here someplace. You don't need to worry about your horse. My uncle is good with horses."

"It's not the horse I'm worried about. It's your uncle. Blackie doesn't like some people riding him and can be very difficult."

Uneasily, Patricia looked down at Tim. "But that native. . . your friend was riding him."

Tim made a sound between a laugh and a groan. "Jackie knows Blackie better than I do. He was a foal from my old horse, and Jackie's helped me care for him since he was born."

Patricia gnawed on her lip uncertainly. "My uncle should be able to manage him. He is very experienced with horses." She saw the question in Tim's eyes and added swiftly to change the subject, "Are you sure not even a shepherd lives near here at times?"

"Land around here does belong to a Mr. Richards, and farther still there's a Mr. Suttor who runs cattle," Tim answered. "I'm not sure just where their boundaries are. But no one lives here. I've never heard of so much as a shepherd's hut in this immediate area. This part of the country is very isolated."

"We were told in Bathurst there was a shepherd living somewhere along the Turon River," Patricia explained, gratified to have steered the conversation away from any personal questions about her and Andy.

Tim stared at her doubtfully and then murmured gently,

"This is certainly the Turon, but it runs through quite a large area before it flows into the Macquarie. It's also very difficult country to be searching for anyone."

Patricia could see the questions forming in his eyes again, so she added hurriedly, "Don't talk now. You must rest. I'll get you another drink."

When she returned, Tim was lying with his eyes closed. The feverish spots of color on each cheek had returned. She knew his leg must be paining him, but he again refused any rum.

"My mother and father never allowed alcohol in our home," he murmured.

"Sounds like mine," Patricia blurted out with a wistful smile. "We did keep a bottle strictly for medicine, but Ma always claimed alcohol was too often the devil's tool to take men's willpower from doing what God wanted them to do."

Tim's eyes widened. "That sounds like something my father would have said."

His eyes clouded with pain, and Patricia sensed that this reaction was from a far deeper wound than the one her bullet had caused. Hoping to take his mind off such sad memories, she asked, "How come you have an aborigine you claim as a friend?"

"Jackie?" Tim was silent for a long moment and then said slowly, "I've known him ever since I was a boy living on Stevens Downs. He was working then for the Gordons, neighbors to the Waverleys."

He was silent once more, and she prompted him by inquiring, "Stevens Downs?"

Tim was so still that she thought he must have dozed off. Then he murmured, "It's a beautiful place—flat fertile plains as far as the eye can see. Stevens Downs is a large sheep station out past Wellington, and my family's first home in Australia. My father worked there from the time he was transported until he—"

"Transported!"

The eyes he turned on her horrified face were fierce with

pride. "Yes, transported. My father was shipped off to a penal colony to serve a ten-year sentence for participating in rioting and destruction of property. He had been foolish enough to want to make a better life for his wife and son, but he trusted the wrong people. They merely used him for their own political agenda. Timothy Hardy was a convict, but he was the most courageous, honest, and humble man you could ever meet. He was also the most loving and faithful Christian anyone could be. He was also. . .also the most wonderful father. . . ." His voice choked and he flung an arm up across his eyes.

Was. That said it all. She recognized Tim's pain as the mirror of her sorrow whenever she thought of her beautiful Irish mother with the fiery hair and temper and love enough for the whole wide world.

"My mother was also loving and faithful. She tried to teach us about. . .about being a good Christian," she murmured sadly. Distressed to see Tim so upset, Patricia instinctively reached out and touched him, stroking his head, his hand, trying to find the right word to offer him comfort. He tensed and flung her hand off.

At Patricia's little gasp of dismay, Tim looked regretful. "Sorry," he murmured huskily. "It's this place. My father died not far from here. It has thrown me off balance, I'm afraid. It. . .it's the first time I've mentioned Father to anyone since Adam, Kate, and their two children departed for England, leaving me in charge of Waverley."

His voice faded away. Tim stared into space, and Patricia thought she had never seen such pain or emptiness on anyone's face before.

The cross. It must have been there that his father had died.

Patricia swallowed and said quickly, "Then let's talk about something else. Tell me about this Adam and Kate or perhaps this Waverley."

He looked at her, and she added a little desperately, "No, no. Blackie. Tell me about your horse."

He studied her face and then to her relief smiled slightly.

"All right, let's talk about Blackie. He was born on Waverley while I was studying in Sydney. He is the foal from one of my father's horses."

Her eyes widened. "You went to school in Sydney?"

He scowled. "Yes, and I hated it, but Kate and Adam insisted that it was what my father had wanted and been planning for me, a decent education."

Kate and Adam again. She would dearly love to know more about them but said instead, "My mother taught us as best she could, but I would have loved to have gone to a school with other children. After. . .after the Indian raid, Pa moved us to another ranch in a safer area, but there was no more chance for formal schooling."

Patricia's face was wistful, and Tim judged her more beautiful than ever. He thought of his own mother, the indomitable Molly Hardy.

"My mother taught me to read and write too," he murmured softly, "but after she died, Father insisted I go to Kate's school for the station hands' children at Waverley." He saw Patricia glance at him a little apprehensively and added swiftly, "She and my little sister, Jane, died from a fever a few years before Father. I've lived with Kate and Adam ever since."

Her eyes widened in dismay and then filled with compassion.

Tim studied her carefully. What was it about this woman's soft, expressive face that made him want to talk about his family for the first time in such a long, long time? "Tell me about your family, Patricia," he asked softly.

She glanced at Tim and then away, staring toward the campfire. "We lived in Ireland when I was little," she said at long last. "Andy is my mother's brother. He went to America before I was born but from time to time sent glowing letters home to my mother and father about the opportunities there. In the end, they decided life was far too hard in Ireland and sailed to New York."

Patricia gave a short laugh. "If anything, life was harder in the big city for most Irish immigrants than the troubles they had left behind in beautiful Ireland. By then Andy was a cowboy. Eventually we managed to track him down and moved west to join him. The plan was to grab some land and set up a ranch together. We eventually ended up in California."

Tim watched the play of emotions on her face as she fell silent. He had heard stories of the hardships the pioneers in America had encountered as they had pushed the frontier farther west. Obviously some of her memories were far from pleasant.

"Were you there when the gold was discovered?" he prompted softly.

She turned her head swiftly and stared at him. He frowned. For a moment he thought he saw something like fear in her eyes, but why would she be afraid?

Glancing away, she said briefly, "Yes, but we lived some distance away. Our ranch was pretty well established before then. Andy and Pa had been very successful raising horses as well as cattle. The horses sold well to the army."

Her voice caught on a little gasp. She looked up at him, studying his face for a long moment. At last she added quietly, "Times were very difficult after Ma died. Some of the men we employed joined the army, and then just after the war with Mexico finished, others headed off to try their luck on the gold fields."

She paused, staring into the distance. Her shoulders were hunched, her voice strained and low when she added harshly, "I've seen only too well how the thought of discovering gold and riches—more than an ordinary man could make in a lifetime—can turn the most sane of men crazy."

The old chestnut horse gave a long whinny. They turned and saw the horse staring in the direction Andy had disappeared earlier, her ears pricked forward. Then they both heard the answering call of a horse and the clatter of hooves.

"Sounds like your uncle's back," Tim said abruptly. He moved restlessly, trying to peer into the bush.

Patricia scrambled to her feet. She was frowning. "But it's

not that long since he left. Andy said—oh, no!" She ran toward the black horse that had come into sight.

Tim heaved himself painfully forward until he could see. Blackie was walking slowly along the creek toward them. He shied away from Patricia as she approached, tossed his head, and started trotting away. She stopped. Tim let out a piercing whistle and saw Blackie pause and swing around, searching for him. He whistled again, and Blackie took a few steps forward, tossing his head up and down. Tim frowned. Blackie was very nervous.

He heard Patricia's soft, crooning voice as she started edging toward the horse. After several attempts, she managed to grab Blackie's reins, and following a brief tussle, she led the horse back to the camp. As she neared, Tim could see Patricia was pale, battling to keep her voice calm in order to reassure the horse.

"Blackie probably just got away from Andy," he said swiftly.

"No," she croaked. "Andy's too experienced a horseman to let one toss him off or to fail to secure one properly."

"Blackie can be pretty unpredictable, but something has certainly frightened him. He's trembling," Tim said slowly, wondering if the hot-tempered Irishman could have harmed the horse. He dismissed the thought immediately. Andy had shown his affection and care for animals, even the big old cart horse.

"Would. . .would the aborigines. . . ?"

"No, they will be long gone," Tim reassured the white-faced woman, hoping fervently he was right.

Patricia stared at him. Then she turned, swiftly unsaddling Blackie before tying him up near the other horses. She strode into the tent. When she reappeared, her revolver was once more strapped to her waist and a rifle rested in her hand. The resolve on her grim face increased Tim's alarm. Before he could speak, she hurried off in the direction from which Blackie had come.

Tim bit off words of caution. Admiration for Patricia's courage and determination warred with his concern for her. Perhaps it had been their shared memories of godly, praying mothers, perhaps his horrible feeling of helplessness. Whatever the reason, as she disappeared from sight, he did something he had not done for far too long.

"Oh, God," Tim pleaded, "keep her safe. Help her find her uncle and bring them back. And please. . ." He paused as his wretched shivering started to subside and the fever once more began heating up his body. "Please," he whispered, "this is no time for me to be sick and leave her to cope alone. Please heal me! Don't let me get any worse."

There was nothing left to do but crawl back inside the tent to his rough bed and wait.

five

Patricia found Andy beside the river, not far from the old landslide and the area where Tim had not wanted to camp.

She heaved a sigh of relief when she first saw her uncle, but her anxiety increased as she raced closer. He made no effort to stand, remaining seated while holding his right arm tightly against his body with his other hand. The face he turned toward her was lined with pain.

"Andy," she gasped breathlessly as she reached him, "what happened?"

He nodded his head toward the cliff behind him and said through gritted teeth, "Thought I'd go and have a look at that."

Patricia stared up the sharp pile of dirt and rocks to where the neat cross had been nailed to the white bark of the old gum tree. "So you saw it too," she said sharply.

He nodded. "Wanted to see what was carved on it."

She hesitated, but it was for Tim to tell Andy about his father if he wanted to. Crouching down beside her uncle, she studied him anxiously.

"You fell from up there? Are you hurt bad?"

"Stupid horse shied at a snake just as I was getting off him."

"A snake!"

Andy saw her glance swiftly around and snorted. "A black one and long gone."

"And Blackie threw you!"

Andy reared his head proudly and glared at her. "He did nothing of the sort! I fell. And no," he added more forcefully and even less truthfully, "I'm not hurt bad. The reins some-how twisted around my arm. Almost wrenched my arm off when the horse jumped back."

She gave an exclamation of distress. "You could have

53

landed on the snake. Here, let me help you up."

Andy groaned and then snapped, "Why do you think I'm still sitting here? Can't stand on my leg. Landed on the side of my foot."

Patricia stared at him speechlessly.

"Don't think anything's broken," he added swiftly. "If you give me a shoulder to lean on, reckon I can make it."

After swiftly examining him, Patricia concluded that while he hadn't broken any bones, he had certainly given the muscles of his ankle, shoulder, and arm a battering. She helped him up, and the two slowly worked their way back to Tim.

Patricia and Andy were thoroughly exhausted when they at last stumbled into camp. A very worried Tim Hardy managed to limp forward a few steps to meet them, but Patricia noted the perspiration on his face and the brightly flushed cheeks that stood in sharp contrast to the paleness of the rest of his face.

There was no choice but to let him help them. She gasped out how Andy had come to grief, omitting any mention of the memorial cross. Once Andy was lying down, she almost fell down herself. She gratefully accepted the cup of water Tim gave her. Andy already had a cup to his lips, and she hoped his wasn't mere water. He, too, needed the only painkiller they had.

The thought almost made her panic. Alone in the Australian bush, she was now responsible for two injured men. Even as she stared at Tim, he swayed, then sank down onto the ground beside them, shivering violently.

"Oh, Tim," she cried, "your leg. . ."

Through chattering teeth he mumbled, "Sorry, Pat. Afraid I'm not going to be much more help to either of you for awhile. I did manage to keep the fire going."

Once she had persuaded Tim to lie back down in the tent, Patricia attended to Andy, grateful that Tim had placed water on the campfire to heat. She put hot packs on Andy's shoulder and ankle and was immensely relieved when gradually, with the help of a few more swallows of rum, the gray, pinched look started to fade from his wrinkled face.

Patricia got little sleep that night. She sponged Tim down when the fever swept through him and piled the blankets on when he started to shiver. Andy also spent a painful night despite her attempts to ease the pain with rags soaked in hot water. Both men tried several times to persuade Patricia to seek her own bed. Both men failed.

At last when soft snores came from Andy's pile of blankets, Tim pretended to be asleep. To his relief, Patricia curled up on her own bedding. He heard her sigh of relief and almost immediately knew she was asleep. After a few moments he raised his head cautiously to make sure she had pulled a blanket over herself, only to see that Andy also had raised his head slightly to peer at Patricia. The two men stared at each other over her sleeping body. Andy's white teeth gleamed in the faint light from the campfire for a moment. Tim grinned in response and then relaxed.

Sheer exhaustion made Tim doze off and on. When he was awake, he heard Andy tossing with discomfort. But whenever Patricia stirred, only gentle snores came from both men. When the long night was at last over, both men paid for their deceit. Andy's muscles were stiff and sore, and Tim's fever was worse. They spent another miserable day.

Patricia cared for them as best she could with the pitiful supplies she had. That night, Tim's fever was no better, and in the light of the new day, his wound looked even worse. Andy forced himself to move around, trying to loosen his strained muscles despite Patricia's white-faced protests.

When Patricia finally left for the creek to get more water, Tim discovered why Andy had not been content to rest. "We've got to get out of here," Andy told him abruptly as soon as she was out of sight. "Pat's exhausted, our food supplies are running low, and you need that leg seen to in better surroundings. It's going bad."

Tim regarded him. He knew Andy had started to respect him for the way he tried to spare Patricia as much as possible.

"Why have you dragged a young woman like Pat out into this wilderness, Andy?" Tim asked abruptly. "And without adequate supplies?"

Anger flashed across the older man's face. "None of your business. We had enough supplies for two people," he snapped, "and it would have lasted much longer if I'd been able to get out these last few days and go hunting."

"Hunting?" Tim's eyes narrowed. "And what would you have been hunting out here?"

At Tim's sharp tones, Andy stiffened. "Well, it wouldn't have been your precious cattle, that's for sure," he snapped, "and for your information she has dragged me here, not the other way around."

"To look for someone called Danny?"

Andy glared at him. "As I said, that's none of your business!" He swallowed, glanced toward the creek, and added hurriedly, "Look, we've got to persuade her we are well enough to tackle the trip to that place you come from unless there's somewhere closer."

"Waverley is the only place for many miles. And I'm well enough." Tim's brave words were belied by the perspiration dripping from his flushed face.

Andy's grin flashed. "Neither of us are, but we've got to get her to a place where she has help and can rest." Worry creased his brow. "Will there be others at your place who could take over your care? She's been living on nerves for too long as it is, and if I'm not careful, she's going to collapse."

Tim thought of the beautiful stone homestead that Elizabeth Waverley's father had built his wife and only daughter. Since they had bought it, Adam and Kate had made it even more comfortable, extending the gardens and orchards, employing more staff. It was indeed a home, a place to relax. Patricia would be able to rest there.

His lips tightened as he remembered the only drawback to the place. Mrs. Wadding. From the start he had not been sure if his new housekeeper and cook would fit in at Waverley.

There had been little choice but to employ the woman temporarily after dear, comfortable old Mrs. Cook had been forced to leave abruptly to care for her seriously ill daughter back in Sydney. Since the transportation of convicts had ceased, servants were becoming harder and harder to find, especially so far from Sydney.

Tim had tried to convince himself how fortunate he had been that Mrs. Wadding was in Bathurst looking for work the very day he had driven Kate's old housekeeper there to help her on her way. Certainly, the woman had been all eagerness to please at first and obviously surprised and even awed by the grandeur of Waverley. She seemed capable enough, but a few times Tim suspected she was far too hard on the girls who helped in the house. They had so quickly lost their smiling faces and cheerful greetings, and the stockmen began to avoid going to the homestead.

When Mrs. Wadding had discovered Tim was not the son of the owner, that his father had been merely a convict, her attitude toward him had changed, often bordering on insolence. The pleasant atmosphere he had always taken for granted at Waverley rapidly deteriorated. He had been only too glad to join the other men in looking for the cattle, but he knew that if Mrs. Cook did not return soon, he would be forced to go to Bathurst and find a replacement for Mrs. Wadding. Kate and Adam would be coming home soon, and the last thing he wanted was for them to return to such an unhappy household.

"Right," Tim said decisively, "we'll go this morning. Between us we should cope."

Relief lit up Andy's face. "Sure we'll cope. We're excellent actors, although I think you need to work on your snoring," he noted, his eyes twinkling. "Besides, between the two of us, don't we have three good hands and two good legs? Although yours might be a bit feeble awhile yet."

Tim grinned. "I'd better work on getting stronger then."

Andy chuckled in appreciation, and soon both men were

laughing out loud. Tim found himself liking Andy immensely.

"Right then," Andy said cheerfully. "Let's start breaking camp before she gets back."

Between them, they managed to roll up the bedding and get some of the tent ropes untied.

"Stop! What are you doing?" Panic laced Patricia's voice. She dropped the water container and rushed toward Andy, who was trying to undo the last rope.

"It's time we moved on," Andy said briefly, but he glanced at Tim before scowling at her. "Tim needs more help than we can get him here, and we are fast running out of food."

Patricia put her hands on her hips and glanced from Andy to Tim, who had just managed to finish tying up a bundle Andy had dragged to him. He straightened and swayed. Abruptly, he fell back down. There was no need to act. The little he had attempted had exhausted him.

"Tim's still too sick," she cried out. "And what happened to all that 'live off the land' talk of yours?"

"Can't hold a rifle well enough," Andy muttered, "and with this bad leg, I couldn't get near enough to get a kangaroo in the sights anyway."

Tim tried to smile at her as he gasped breathlessly, "Just. . . bit weak. Been in bed. . .too long."

"And you should still be in bed," she cried out, rushing over to him. "Andy, look at him!"

Tim started to push himself up from the ground but fell back with a disgusted groan. "Sorry, Mate," he mumbled to Andy. "More lessons will have to wait. Done all. . .can for a bit."

Andy used the piece of wood he had selected from the pile of firewood as a crutch and limped painfully over to them. "Then we'll make a bed in the dray for us to share."

Patricia looked from one to the other.

"We have to get out of here, Patty dear," Andy said quietly, "or we'll all get weaker without enough to eat. We can take it slowly, but we have to start moving."

Patricia stared at her uncle. "You only call me that when. . .

You're very serious aren't you?"

Andy nodded silently.

"I—I could try and trap or shoot something myself," she faltered.

Tim shook his head. "Isn't much wildlife in the immediate area," he said. "I agree with your uncle. It would be much better to go to Waverley. On the way we might even meet some of the stockmen. They should have arrived home already with the cattle and discovered I hadn't made it back. They. . .they wouldn't look for me here."

Because I never come to this place where the memory of Father's death still haunts me.

Patricia stared at Tim and then back at Andy. "Right," she said reluctantly. Andy started to bend down to pick up the bedding, and she added hastily, "Only as long as you let me do the heavy bits and you men rest when you should."

She grabbed the bundle from Andy and hefted it into the cart. Swiftly she spread the bedding out to form a rough bed. When she turned around, she thought she caught Andy winking at Tim, but their smiles quickly disappeared and Andy started slowly back to the tent. She stared after him suspiciously, but she felt too pleased that the men were getting along to pursue the matter.

"I'm packing my own gear," she called out rapidly, "as well as the cooking things. That way I'll know where everything is when we stop next."

Only when she picked up the pan that she usually cooked on but that she had used to pan the riverbed did she remember the gold dust. She had hidden it carefully in the battered old bag that held her few pieces of clothing.

Patricia hesitated, wondering if she should show it to Andy. A small amount, it was probably only what the miners called "fool's gold" anyway. She shrugged. Getting help for Tim and Andy was far more important. But she looked around, taking careful note of the hills that rose a little way back from the creek, looking for landmarks to help them find this creek again. Perhaps when they found Danny, they might be able to come back and explore this region. And they could use that cross on the tree to make sure they were in the right place.

Despite her protests, both men helped her more than she considered wise. Tim had to rest frequently, but it took all three to harness the horse to the cart and tie the chestnut and Blackie to the back of it.

Two Irish tempers exploded when Patricia refused to let Andy drive the cart. At first Tim was alarmed by their fiery words, but at last he shrugged and closed his eyes, glad to rest on his makeshift bed in the cart until the battle was over. When Patricia won the day by jumping up and sitting in the driver's seat, completely ignoring her spluttering uncle, Tim chuckled softly at them.

At last they were on their way. As the dray jolted slowly over the rough ground, Tim grabbed his leg, his teeth clenched from pain. He had tried to give them directions to Waverley, and he fervently hoped they found the road before he succumbed to the pain and his worsening fever.

Three excruciating days passed as they made their way to Tim's home. His infection had refused to go away, and he knew Patricia was desperately worried about the state of his leg by the time the Waverley homestead came into view, nestled in its setting of pine trees and tall gums.

Through a haze of pain and weakness, Tim heard Patricia's sharp exclamation. "Is. . .is that really Waverley?" she gasped. "Why, it's beautiful!" Astonishment and something like awe sounded in her voice.

"Yes," Tim managed weakly, "but it's still not Stevens Downs."

He saw Patricia glance at him sharply. Had he told her about his old home, about the horizon that stretched for miles without a hill in sight? As much as he loved Waverley, those never-ending plains had always called to something deep inside him, something he wasn't even sure he understood.

The last stretch to the house was not as rough as the bush

track, but not far from the house, a wheel hit a rut in the side of the road. Pain slashed through Tim's leg. He could not stop the groan that slipped past his lips.

"Careful, Girl. You went off the road there," Andy admonished sharply. "Here, let me take over this last bit or you'll land us in that ditch. You're exhausted."

After that, things were confused for Tim. He thought he must have passed out for several minutes. He came to when he heard a woman screaming, "Oh, you wicked, wicked people! What have you done to poor Mr. Hardy? You've killed him!"

Tim groaned. "Be quiet, you stupid woman," he started to mutter, but his voice was drowned out by Andy's voice saying that very thing.

"Good man," he whispered approvingly and let the darkness descend.

The next few days were a blur. There were strident tones and rough hands until he heard Andy's roar once more. Then to his relief, she was there. Her hands were gentle, easing the pain in his leg, her tones soothing him to rest.

And then her voice raised in fury roused him. She was ordering someone to get out. He forced his eyes open and peered curiously at a red-faced, plump man retreating before her. Mrs. Wadding screeched again, but the sound was shut out as the door slammed.

"Pat?" he croaked.

"Yes, Tim, I'm here," her voice whispered.

"Don't. . .go. . ."

"I'm not going anywhere," she said in a choked voice and then vehemently added, "And neither are you!"

He wondered vaguely where she thought he might go, but then her face loomed closer. Soft lips touched his forehead. Comforted, he smiled and went to sleep.

ᕼ

Patricia wiped furiously at the tears streaming down her face as she collapsed into the chair beside Tim's bed. She shuddered as she heard more shouting and screaming from somewhere in the house. Then she identified the thud of the big cedar front door followed by the rattle of horse and carriage.

A few moments later, Andy limped into the room. His face was red with anger, his eyes fiery.

"Has the doctor gone?" she whispered.

"Yes, and good riddance to him," he said in controlled tones.

Patricia gave a broken laugh. "Poor Tim. He told me house-keepers are very hard to come by out here. I don't know what he is going to think about us upsetting his so much. She was furious enough when we banned her from Tim's bedroom after he became so agitated every time she came near him. Now she is utterly scandalized, certain we are letting Tim. . . letting Tim. . ." She choked on a sob, unable to put into words what the woman had screamed as Andy had bundled the pompous, incompetent doctor from the house.

Andy drew her head against his comforting shoulder. "But we know we are doing nothing less than saving that young man from a fool," he stated vehemently. "When Tim comes to, if he's anything like the young man I'm thinkin' he is, he'll agree with our decision." His Irish accent had increased, indicating just how upset he was.

"Oh, Andy dear! What if we're wrong? What if. . . ?"

"We aren't wrong," he interrupted her anguished whisper, adding with grim determination, "but we've got much work to do to prove it. Let's get started."

Two days passed before Patricia knew they had won the battle to keep Tim Hardy alive after refusing to allow the doctor to amputate his leg.

Andy found Patricia in her bedroom, sobbing her heart out with sheer relief.

She raised a beaming face to him. "Oh, Andy, he's going to be all right. He spoke quite lucidly to me, and now he's sleeping more soundly than he has since. . .since. . . I've been so afraid we made the wrong decision not letting that doctor. . ." She stopped, not able to voice the horrible recommendation the doctor had made.

Andy hugged her and let her cry all over him until her tears dried up at last.

A few more days passed before Tim was well enough to be told about the doctor and to be informed that his housekeeper was not speaking to either Patricia or Andy, refusing even to cook for them or let the maids clean their rooms.

At first Tim was furious. "And you didn't make her leave with the doctor?" he exclaimed.

Andy chuckled. "Can't say I wasn't tempted! She will never know how close she came to being tied up and bundled into that buggy with him."

Tim looked from Andy's defiant face to Patricia's apprehensive one, and his scowl lifted. He grinned at them. "Pity you didn't. They could have driven each other crazy all the way to Bathurst. What stopped you?"

"We couldn't look after this place as well as care for you," Andy said bluntly. Tim looked at Patricia's exhausted face with concern, and Andy added swiftly, "Afraid I also didn't have the authority if—"

He stopped abruptly, and Patricia knew that deep down Andy had also been afraid Tim might have died.

"It would have been good riddance," Tim said weakly.

He reached out and took Patricia's hand, holding it as tightly as he could. Looking into her tear-filled eyes, he whispered a fervent thank-you. He looked over at Andy and smiled gratefully.

Then he turned back and smiled so tenderly at her that Patricia knew her heart was in grave danger. No matter how often she told herself she did not know Tim well enough, her heart risked giving itself to the thin, pale man she had prayed and wept over until they had won him back from the very gates of death.

six

Tim remained thin and weak for some time, but Andy and Patricia were amazed by how rapidly his general health improved. He insisted on getting out of bed long before Patricia thought he was ready to do so. Certainly he did not stay up very long those first couple times, but each day he steadily improved until he only needed to rest for an hour or so each day. After that first morning they had talked to Tim, Patricia found herself gently but firmly banned from Tim's bedroom until he was dressed.

When she protested, Andy dropped into the exaggerated Irish brogue he liked to adopt at times. "Now, me darlin', it's a very proper young man it is." He paused, his eyes twinkling mischievously, before adding, "Tim is already embarrassed enough you have been so intimately caring for him all this time. And he doesn't want to give that there sour Mrs. Wadding any more juicy bits of scandal." The smile disappeared, and he became very much the stern, protective uncle. "Nor does he want to risk damaging your reputation!"

She gaped at Andy. Did she have any reputation left? According to one of Mrs. Wadding's tirades, Patricia was nothing more than a "hussy dressed in men's clothes, and no better than she should be!" Patricia had been thankful Andy had not heard that particular session with the housekeeper, or Mrs. Wadding might have found herself summarily dispatched back to Bathurst after all. And Patricia had acknowledged to herself that she was far too exhausted to take over the running of the large house as well as supervise the food for the stockmen's quarters.

Once she was not so consumed with Tim's hour-by-hour care, Patricia made it her business to sort out her and Andy's clothes and bedding. Despite the scorn directed her way by Mrs. Wadding, she washed and cleaned their things, glad to get rid of the dust from their travels and camping. Andy grumbled at his niece's burst of energy but helped lift the heavy buckets of hot water and baskets of laundry for her when Mrs. Wadding made sure the other servants were too busy to help. Patricia disdained accepting assistance, but because bouts of deep weariness swept over her from time to time, she was secretly glad of Andy's help.

The days, and then the weeks slipped by. Except for Mrs. Wadding's unpleasantness, Patricia found herself relaxing in the peace of Waverley.

Andy soon became restless and often wandered down to the stables or sheds, chatting with any station hand around. The men out with Tim had not arrived back until several days after Tim was well on the road to recovery. The drought conditions provided little feed for the herd and slowed the return to Waverley. Apparently only one man had made a brief search for Tim, the conclusion being reached that Tim had returned to Waverley by himself.

Andy had shaken his head at their slackness and lack of care, but he enjoyed discussing with the stockmen the differences between running a ranch in America and the Australian cattle and sheep station. As his injuries healed, there were soon plenty of tasks around the place he willingly helped out with.

Although they had discovered Jackie was Tim's main offsider, he still did not put in an appearance. When Patricia mentioned that to Tim, he merely shrugged and said with resignation that Jackie would get back from his walkabout when he was ready. It could be weeks—even months—before Jackie's aboriginal business was completed.

Patricia and Tim spent many hours sitting quietly together, reading, and playing games. At first they sat in Tim's bedroom, but as he improved, they graduated to the parlor or study. Once he was well enough, he insisted on going outside, long before Patricia thought he should.

"Four walls have always stifled me," he explained, giving an endearing smile to his petite nurse.

She stared at him doubtfully. Certainly his cheeks were filling out again. Plenty of healthy color now brightened the lean face tanned and wrinkled by hours spent in the outdoors. Her heart stirred again. It was a handsome face, a strong face with steady, thoughtful amber eyes. The light brown hair, now needing a trim, had the most beguiling wave in it. That lock of hair had fallen across his forehead again. So many times she had smoothed it back when he was ill.

In the end she agreed to let Tim sit on the verandah. Eventually she allowed him to take a small walk in the garden, leaning on her arm and an old walking stick. Those walks gradually became longer as Tim's strength returned.

A little diffidently at first, but with increasing confidence, Patricia and Timothy talked about many things that they had never shared with anyone else. They told each other stories about their parents, the adventures of sailing and settling in a new country, the lessons about God and faith their parents had tried to teach them.

After a few weeks, Tim found himself telling Patricia about that dark day his father had died. It had not been something Tim had intended or planned to share with her. They had been sitting on the verandah watching the sun display its glorious colors as it sank beneath the horizon of undulating hills. Their friendship had developed to the point that telling her seemed natural.

Patricia watched Tim's face, listening silently as he poured out his heart to her. As he started to describe those last moments he had held his father, Tim faltered and stopped.

Tears filled her eyes. She simply reached out and held his hands tightly in her own. Then she quietly told him about the time her mother had been shot by that first arrow launched before any of them had been aware of the small group of Indians creeping up on their small farm. Fortunately both Andy and her father had been home and had quickly fought off the Indians, but it had taken several days and nights before her mother had finally succumbed to her wound. After that, her father and Andy had sold up, moving to a more settled area where the Indians were friendlier.

Somehow, in that quiet corner of the garden under a massive flowering peach tree, it seemed perfectly natural for Tim to put his arm around Patricia. Pink petals gently floated down and settled on the white daisies at their feet. When she finished speaking, they were still for a few moments, her head resting on his shoulder.

At last she sighed and started to sit up, saying quietly, "Well, it was a long time ago now for both of us, and life has gone on since then."

Tim softly smoothed back a stray piece of hair from her beautiful face.

She turned impulsively toward him. "I haven't mentioned Danny yet. He. . ."

Tim hardly heard what she said. He was watching her, staring into her expressive eyes that never ceased to fascinate him. She paused. A look of startled surprise, of awareness, filled her face. Her adorable lips, so close to his, opened slightly. A deep flush spread across her face.

She was absolutely irresistible.

They were so close he only had to move those last few inches. Gently, ever so gently they explored each other's lips. They withdrew, exchanged a look of startled wonder, and then kissed again. Tim's arms slipped around her. Her hands reached behind his neck to hold him closer to her.

It was bliss.

It was sheer heaven.

"Mr. Hardy! Miss! How could you?" The screech froze them.

They tore apart.

Mrs. Wadding was staring at them in absolute horror. "I knew it," she screeched, "taking advantage of a poor ill man!"

Tim swallowed, feeling the heat flood into his face. He

glanced at Patricia. Her fingers were on those luscious lips he had just tasted. Her face was white as a sheet. But her eyes were looking behind Mrs. Wadding, staring at her uncle as he came running toward them across the lawn.

"What is it? What's wrong?" he barked.

"That wicked, wicked girl," wailed Mrs. Wadding. "She's been. . .been. . .oh, the shame of her! And you such a Christian gentleman, Mr. Hardy!"

Tim came to his senses. Fury took over from his first anguish at having the wonderful moment torn to pieces. "Mrs. Wadding," he roared, "that is enough! Be quiet, Woman!"

Something in his face made the woman take a step back. She opened her mouth, but Tim was not finished.

"If you say one more word. . .one word," he spluttered, "I will put you on a horse and have you off Waverley in the next moment."

She stood there. Her gaze darted from Tim to a glowering Andy. She tossed her head and stomped away.

"What's going on here?"

Patricia was still staring at Tim in bemusement. At Andy's abrupt question, she turned to confront her uncle.

Tim started to say, "Sir, I'm afraid—"

"It is absolutely none of your business, Andy!" Patricia interrupted fiercely.

Andy stared at her. His gaze dropped to her lips. Scarlet flooded into her face, but she tilted her chin and stared back at him with haughty challenge.

Tim felt a flood of relief as Andy relaxed. He thought a twinkle briefly flickered in Andy's eyes, but then his expression hardened again as he turned to Tim.

"Anything that happens to you is very much my business, Patty darling, especially when your own father is so far away from here," Andy murmured softly. His gaze became menacing as he looked at Tim with much the expression Tim had seen when they first met over the barrels of Andy's two revolvers. "You do understand that, don't you, Mr. Hardy?"

Tim stared back at the man angrily for a long moment. He nodded ever so slightly. "I believe your niece is very privileged to have you to care what happens to her, Sir," he said crisply.

He glanced at Patricia, who watched them with apprehension. Tim smiled at her gently, comfortingly, before turning back to Andy O'Donnell. Tim looked at him steadily. The men had become quite good friends, but he knew that Andy would not put anything above his niece's welfare. "I can assure you that I will do everything in my power to see that nothing happens to her," Tim stated firmly.

Patricia gave an embarrassed moan, turned, and fled.

Tim took a step toward her, then stopped. His head high, he turned back to Andy, who was watching the fleeing woman thoughtfully.

When he looked back at Tim, the two men studied each other for a long moment.

"See that you keep that promise, Lad," Andy murmured before striding after his niece.

Tim deeply regretted things remained strained between Patricia and himself for several days. He realized how much talking to her about his father had helped melt away a lot of his pain and sense of loss. Tim hoped she too had been helped, but there were times after the strain had eased at last, that he knew she was holding back from him, holding him at a distance especially when any mention of their families came up.

❧

Patricia was so thankful when she and Tim at last regained their old easy friendship. She wanted to tell him about Danny, came so close to doing so, but Danny's very life might depend on her keeping his secret. And she had promised him so faithfully not to say a word to anyone. She had already broken that promise when she had told Andy.

As the days flew past, Tim and Patricia in unspoken agreement refused to let the sadness and wounds each carried deep in their souls to surface, so as not to disturb the fragile relationship developing between them. And if there were moments when Patricia longed for Tim to kiss her again, she gave no sign of it.

Just sitting in each other's presence of an evening and quietly reading together was a delight the two lonely young people savored. A few times they slipped into discussions about faith and what they had been taught about the Bible, God, and how to experience a meaningful relationship with Him.

At other times, Patricia persuaded Tim to tell her more about his father. She was fascinated by his stories, including how young Tim had fallen into the Thames River trying to reach his father as the convicts were being loaded onto their transport ship and how the boy had been rescued by the convict John Martin. On the journey to Australia, Tim's father had been a faithful witness for his Lord to the other convicts. But only one listened to him—the same John Martin. John, a convicted murderer, had often protected the frailer Timothy from the persecution of the other convicts, and eventually John had come to a personal faith in Christ that had transformed him from an angry, despairing young man to a man at peace and with the certain hope that God had his future in His control.

Even more fascinating to Patricia was the story of how Elizabeth Waverley, a passenger returning to Australia, had befriended both convicts on board the ship, believed John's pleas of his innocence, and fallen deeply in love with him. She told Adam Stevens about the two men. Adam had been a convict assigned to Elizabeth's father, who was himself an ex-convict. Adam had worked so faithfully on Waverley for Elizabeth's family that he had been left Stevens Downs in her rich father's will. For Elizabeth's sake, Adam had employed Timothy and had had John assigned to him, never dreaming that he would become so caught up in the lives of the two convicts. Adam, too, had come to believe John Martin's story that he was innocent of the murder he had been convicted of and that he was the rightful heir of a member of the English aristocracy.

"This Kate of yours, Adam's wife, is John Martin's sister,

the daughter of a lord?" Patricia gasped at that part of Tim's story.

Tim nodded, his eyes twinkling at her awe. "Adam traveled to England and met Kate. Together they brought their wicked cousin's schemes to nought, proving that he was the real murderer all along. John Martin is now my Lord Farnley, and Elizabeth Waverley is Lady Farnley," he added in impressive tones.

Patricia gaped at him. He laughed and told her more, of how stubbornly Kate had ignored all Adam's scruples about a man convicted of fraud marrying an earl's daughter until Adam could no longer resist their deep love for each other.

As enjoyable as these conversations were, however, the time Patricia spent with Tim was kept fairly brief, and it was usually Patricia who cut the sessions short. A certain look would cross Tim's face that told her he expected her to tell him more about her family in return for his own stories. She felt desolate, longing to be able to share with him, but not daring to. She hated pushing Tim away when he so naturally wanted to know everything about her as their affection for each other grew.

A couple times Patricia caught an expression of concern in her uncle's eyes when she and Tim were talking or laughing together. Although it had upset her at the time, the little talk Andy had given her after that episode in the garden made far too much sense. She was glad Andy had held his peace since, not putting into words what she knew only too well to be true. Her home and responsibilities were a long way from this quiet valley in New South Wales.

And there was still Danny.

As Tim became stronger, he gradually became busier with running the property. Patricia deliberately spent less time with him. She became quieter, more withdrawn.

Andy went searching for her one day when he knew Tim was busy catching up on the paperwork that had been accumulating. Patricia was sitting in the shade of the verandah, staring out across the homestead garden toward the west. She glanced up at Andy as his boots clumped toward her and swiftly wiped a hand across her wet cheeks.

Her uncle sank down on one of the chairs near her and took her hand. They stared out across the paddocks. It had been a hot day, a foretaste of the summer almost upon them.

After a long silence, she sighed and said softly, "It's time to go, isn't it?"

Andy squeezed her hand understandingly before letting it go. "Yes," he said abruptly, "long past time." After a pause he added, "The stockman arrived back from Bathurst a little while ago."

Something in his voice brought her sad gaze back to him. At the look on his face, she exclaimed, "Danny?"

Andy nodded. "The stockman brought word that a few weeks back someone called Sean McMurtrie had been asking all kinds of questions about any stories of gold being found in the Bathurst, Wellington, area. They think he headed west."

"That was the name Danny used in California. What we were told by that other old man must be true. He headed out this way to try to find gold."

Patricia closed her eyes, waiting for the rush of excitement that should come at the confirmation that Danny was indeed in this part of New South Wales.

It didn't come. Instead she fought threatening tears at the thought of saying good-bye to this place that had become a haven. And then there was the young man with light brown hair still bleached by the relentless sun of this land. The young man with that light in his amber eyes that warmed her through and through, who had become so much more than an acquaintance.

"We should leave tomorrow morning, me darlin'."

She slowly stood up, brushing down the skirt of one of the old-fashioned dresses Tim had insisted weeks ago she borrow from an old trunk. When she had murmured her regret at only bringing one skirt from their luggage left in Sydney, he had told Andy to haul the trunk out of a cupboard in a storeroom. It had only taken a few stitches to make a couple fit her perfectly and a careful clean and press before she could wear them. She had been well rewarded by the glow in Tim's eyes as he looked at her. For the first time, she had felt truly beautiful.

"I'll go and pack." Her voice was steady, and she did not look at Andy as she asked quietly, "Have you told Tim?"

"I thought you might like to do that yourself," Andy said a trifle huskily.

"Yes. Thank you. He. . .he's busy now. I'll tell him after tea."

Instead of heading straight to her room, she hesitated for a moment and then hurried down the steps and out into the sunshine for one last look around the garden. It was a blaze of late spring color. Waverley employed a gardener to make sure it was well kept, especially in the dry seasons.

Tears blurred her eyes as she walked aimlessly. At last she reached the gate that opened out onto the road they would take the next morning. She leaned on it, her shoulders hunched, her head bowed.

☙

Tim was never sure what drew his attention away from his books to look out the wide study windows. Watching Patricia walking down the path was far more pleasant than studying his accounts. She had looked absolutely beautiful at breakfast that morning, and he had suddenly realized nothing would make him happier than to be greeted by her smiling face every morning for the rest of his life.

She paused at the gate, staring out across the dry, dusty paddocks, and then bowed her head. He frowned. Something was wrong. She looked unhappy, a very picture of misery. Had Mrs. Wadding upset her again? He knew Patricia took care to hide from him the many mean and petty things the spiteful housekeeper had subjected her to. Despite his inability to go to Bathurst himself, he should have rid Waverley of that woman weeks ago.

Tim jumped up and made his way out of the study, only to

be waylaid by Mrs. Wadding with vicious complaints about not having her supply order filled correctly by the luckless stockman who had been to Bathurst. Without giving Tim a chance to respond, she raved on, listing other misdemeanors committed by the two servant girls.

Then she was foolish enough to start in on Patricia and Andy. "No-hopers, the pair of them," she spat out, "threw poor Dr. Mint out, they did. Refused to let him treat you. It's a miracle you survived. And now throwing herself at you. . .well. . ."

"Quiet, Woman!"

Tim's roar stunned Mrs. Wadding to silence. Only once before had Tim raised his voice to her. He had not mentioned that incident again, but she had severely underestimated him if she thought he had forgotten.

Tim drew himself up and fixed her with an angry glare. "I should have done this that day you so rudely intruded on our privacy in the garden," he ground out. "Seeing you are so dissatisfied with all you have to put up with at Waverley, I believe it is past time we parted company, Mrs. Wadding. Have your bags packed by tomorrow morning, and I will arrange for you to be driven to Bathurst."

Her mouth dropped open, and she went pale. "But you need me. You—"

"You are sadly mistaken, Madam. We certainly do not need your constant carping and poisonous tongue and will manage much better without you."

Fury swept over her narrow face. "I suppose you think that harpy of yours will be able to—"

"That is enough, Mrs. Wadding!" Tim turned his back on the spluttering woman and limped from the house.

Patricia no longer stood at the gate. It hung slightly open, unusual for a woman reared where shutting gates was taught from the time her first steps were taken.

Nevertheless, Tim went around the garden, hoping to find her. Unsuccessful, he returned to the gate and wondered in which direction she might have gone. It took a few minutes before he saw her standing a long way down the driveway, peering up into the branches of the tall gum tree.

He hesitated. His strength was increasing every day, but he had not yet ventured quite so far from the house. A pang went through him. He knew that tree only too well and the steep rise on which it stood.

❧

Walking swiftly up the hill had somehow eased the sharp ache in Patricia's heart. She was sure this was the tree from which Tim had watched the road for his father. It was certainly the tallest one on that rise. As she paused beneath it, she heard a faint mew and looked up. A small kitten crouched on a high branch.

The small animal provided a welcome distraction from her somber thoughts. She called to it, trying to coax it down. It started toward her, then ran out onto a thin limb above her head that bent alarmingly underneath the kitten's weight. Terrified, the animal clung to its precarious perch. The branch swayed up and down, and Patricia expected it to come crashing to the ground at any moment. The kitten mewed frantically.

"Oh, you stupid creature," she sighed. "I suppose you want me to rescue you?"

Patricia had climbed many trees with Danny when they were young. But it had been awhile. This one looked relatively easy. She shrugged, hitched up her skirt, and started up. She could not help thinking of the young Tim sitting in the tree, searching the horizon for a father who never came.

She was quite a long way off the ground when Tim's voice called out breathlessly, "Patricia, whatever are you doing up there?"

She froze and then looked down. He stood directly beneath her, one hand resting on the trunk of the tree.

"There. . .there's a kitten. . . ."

"She'll find her own way down."

Patricia peered around the branch she was clinging to. Sure enough, the kitten had already reached the relative safety of a strong branch just above her. She hesitated, unwilling to retreat without the wretched creature.

"Pat, Darling, do come down out of there!" Tim called anxiously.

Darling? He had been so reserved, as proper as any gentleman could be, since that unforgettable moment in the garden. She had thought he must have regretted it, when she had wanted only to repeat it again and again and—

She gave a little gasp, her breath quickening. And now Tim had called her. . .

Eagerly she started back down the tree, leaving the kitten to its own fate.

Afterward, Patricia could never say what happened for sure. Perhaps the skirt she so seldom wore was her downfall, perhaps it had been her reaction to Tim's endearment. One moment she was several feet from safety, the next her foot slipped and she went crashing down.

She screamed. Tim cried out and sprang forward. She hit him with enough force to send him flat on his back with her in a tangle of petticoats on top of him. For a moment she lay there, the breath knocked from her, and then realized Tim had not moved.

"Tim, your leg!" she cried in dismay, rolling off him.

He lay motionless, blood trickling from where his head had hit the sharp edge of a protruding rock.

"Oh, no! Not again," she moaned.

Once more her foolishness had brought injury to Tim Hardy.

seven

"There, I think he's waking up at last."

Tim wished the man would go away and let him sleep. He was too weary to wake up. He tried to tell him to go away, to let him sleep. All that seemed to want to come out of his mouth was a dry croak. Pain shot through his head.

Someone gave a low, choked sound. He wasn't sure if it was a sob or a chuckle. Soft lips touched his forehead, his cheek.

A woman's voice spoke softly. "But you've had more than enough sleep these last few days, my dear, dear Tim. It is time to wake up now so you can have some broth."

Broth? He hated broth. Tim frowned. The woman sounded anxious. What was she doing in his bedroom? And surely he knew that voice with the Irish lilt, whose lips were so gentle, so loving.

With effort, he opened his eyelids. He was rewarded by the sight of a sweet face and green eyes that sparkled with tears as she smiled down at him.

"Patricia?" he croaked, trying to sit up. A sharp pain pierced the back of his head even as gentle hands reached to prevent him. His head whirling, he fell back on the soft pillow.

"You must lie still," Patricia said urgently.

Tim stared up at her. "You. . .you shot me and. . .and. . ."

She stared and then nodded slowly. The tears started trickling down her face as she whispered, "You'll never forget that, will you?"

He stared at her, trying to remember.

"That time you lost a lot of blood, had a bad fever, but now. . ." Her voice choked and trailed to a stop.

He tried to move a hand up to her. Patricia mustn't cry.

77

At his attempt to move, the pain throbbed again in his shoulder, his head. He closed his eyes, fighting to remember. Images started seeping through him. His leg had been on fire. He had been in the back of a dray. No, no, that had been before. There had been some woman screeching.

"Mrs. Wadding. . .she. . ."

The man's voice said firmly, "She won't be troubling you anymore."

"Andy?"

"Yes, it's me, Lad."

Tim tried to remember. There had been something about a gunshot, then a doctor. No, no, it had been a. . .a tree. . . .

His head filled with pain. Someone gave a muffled sob. Tim frowned and opened his eyes, squinting around. He was in his own comfortable room at Waverley.

A gruff voice said abruptly, "And how many times do I have to tell you to stop feelin' so guilty, me darlin'?"

Tim turned his head a little too swiftly, and Andy's scowling face swam into view.

"That last time this idiot lost a lot of blood because of his own foolishness over those aborigines and even more because of his stubbornness in not telling us. And this last was pure and simply an accident." Andy stopped as he saw Tim looking at him. "Come on now, Lad," he added in a softer voice that belied his scowl, "let's get a couple more pillows under you so you can get some food into you."

"Not. . .not broth."

"Oh dear, and after all the trouble that has been taken to kill the hen and pluck it and cook it," another woman's voice said lightly from near the doorway.

Patricia gave a start and stepped back from his bed.

For a moment Tim thought he must still be crazy from the fever. . .no. . .this time he had hit his head.

"Kate?" he managed, staring at the face that should have been fifteen thousand miles away. He shut his eyes. He must be hallucinating.

From behind her another voice, a very familiar drawl, said loudly, "Well, it's about time you came to and welcomed us home, Tim Hardy."

"Adam?" He jerked his head around, lifting it up to peer toward the doorway. He fell back with a groan from the pain.

"I told you he wasn't well enough yet for you to surprise him," Patricia said crossly, and then her voice lost its sharp edge as she turned back to her patient. "You really mustn't move too quickly just yet, Tim," she admonished him. "Here, have a sip of water."

A gentle hand lifted his head and a cup was held to his dry lips. Suddenly he knew it had been Patricia's hands that he had felt through the haze of pain, her lilting voice that had soothed him during the dark night. Or had there been more than one?

It took an effort to swallow, but the water did relieve his dry mouth and help clear his head a little.

And it *was* Adam and Kate beaming down at him.

"You're home!"

"Yes, only in the last hour, and only to find you've turned the place upside down," Kate said with a smile. She bent down to kiss him, and he saw the caring and concern in her eyes that had warmed his lonely and motherless heart so many times over the years. "And we've brought visitors who are very anxious to see you."

"I really don't think you should bother him too much just yet," that voice with the attractive lilt said sharply. "He has been very ill and was still not fully recovered before. . . before. . ."

"Yes, so we discovered the moment we arrived!" Adam's voice was filled with fury as he glared across the bed at Patricia and Andy.

"Not. . .not her fault," Tim managed.

"Not according to Jackie and that wretched housekeeper who still hasn't stopped screeching about—"

Adam stopped abruptly as Kate raised an urgent hand. "I

thought I said you could only come in here if you didn't disturb him about what has happened."

Patricia moved abruptly, shrinking closer to her uncle, who was glaring back at Adam Stevens. For a moment Tim thought she looked frightened, but then she straightened, tilting her chin and gazing steadily back at Adam.

Tim looked from her to his old friends, still hardly believing that after all those lonely months they had returned from England. Relief swept through him. Everything would be all right at Waverley now that they were here to take charge once more. It had been a huge responsibility.

"Why, Kate. . .Adam. . .you're really home!" he stammered again, holding out his hand. "But how. . .why didn't you let me know? I could have met your ship."

Kate took his hand, saying softly, "We wanted to surprise you, Tim dear. We were in such a rush to get here, we've even left the children in Sydney with friends. But you've surprised us instead. Now, don't try and talk just yet. I'm so sorry you haven't been well, but I'm sure you will be up and about very soon."

She glared at her husband. "And if you can't be trusted not to upset him, you may leave, Mr. Stevens, and not be allowed back here until he can cope with your bossiness."

Tim found himself starting to smile despite his throbbing head. Kate only called her husband that when she was cross with him.

"No," he muttered, "too good to see you again."

That earned him another quick kiss from Kate. "And it is so good to see you, too, my dear boy. But we can all talk more when you are a little stronger." She turned to Patricia and said dismissively, "I'll attend to him now, Miss Casey. You must be tired."

Tim frowned. There had been a sharp note in Kate's voice that he did not like at all.

Patricia, her head still raised, stared at Kate. Then, before he could protest, Patricia turned and strode from the room.

Tim frowned, only then realizing she was wearing her trousers once more.

He looked swiftly toward Andy. The man was scowling savagely at Kate and Adam. Andy opened his mouth and then snapped it shut before following his niece without a glance at Tim.

"I'll see you later when this dragon says you can have visitors," Adam said heartily. A little too heartily.

As the door shut behind him, exhaustion filled Tim. He was ashamed at the feeling of relief the quietness gave. Eagerly he accepted a cup of water from Kate and then endured her fussing with his pillows. Suddenly he remembered other hands ministering to him, coaxing him to swallow some vile drink, bathing his burning face with cool water.

"How long have I been ill?" he muttered urgently.

"Apparently your last injury happened a couple of days ago," Kate said briskly. "Now don't worry about anything until—"

"My last injury. . .a couple of days ago!" Horror swept through Tim as he started to remember more clearly. "The tree. I fell. Patricia, she. . .she. . .was she hurt?" he asked urgently.

Kate made a sound that sounded like a well-bred snort. "Don't worry about that young woman. I have no doubt she can look after herself."

Tim stared at her. What did she mean? What was wrong with Patricia?

He thought hard. The tree had been afterward. His head was aching so much, he couldn't think straight. A faint memory of raised voices came to him. Patricia had been shouting at someone, ordering him from the room.

"She. . .she made the doctor leave," he muttered, still rather confused at what had happened when.

"She did, did she?" There was stern disapproval in Kate's voice.

"He. . .wanted to bleed me. She. . .she told him I'd already lost too much blood. And. . .and there was something else. Oh, yes, he wanted to cut off my foot, but she wouldn't let him." He rubbed a hand to his forehead.

Kate's frown disappeared. She gasped in horror. "Your foot. . .she. . . Well, good for her!"

Kate was silent. After a moment, Tim thought she muttered something that sounded like, "At least she had sense enough for that." Then she added brightly, "I left orders for Mrs. Wadding to prepare some broth for you as soon as you were awake enough to eat. Now if you are comfortable, I'll go and. . .oh!"

"I had already taken the liberty of seeing to the cooking myself, Mrs. Stevens."

Relief swept through Tim at the familiar voice. He raised his head as swiftly as he dared. "Patricia?"

She was looking defiantly at Kate as she came closer. Her eyes were large in her pale face. They turned and searched his face keenly. A relieved smile transformed her.

"You're really better," she said simply. "I'm glad."

He reached out his hand. Disappointment swept through him as she ignored it and looked away. Only then did he see the tray she was carrying as she placed it on a table next to the bed. When she turned back, he held out his hand again. She looked at it and then slowly reached out and clasped it in hers.

"It's not the chicken broth, just some nourishing vegetable soup I've had simmering all day in hopes you'd be well enough at last to manage some," she murmured softly, her eyes down.

He held her hand as tightly as he could. Relief and weariness swept through him in equal measure. "You will stay until we can talk? And Andy?"

Uncertainty filled her face. For the first time, Tim realized just how exhausted Patricia looked. Black circles ringed redstreaked eyes, and she was very pale and drawn.

She bit her lip, glancing briefly toward Kate. "We. . .we

should be on our way now that you have your folk to look after you," she murmured.

Kate cleared her throat and said in a stilted voice, "It was very good of you to prepare the food for Tim, Miss. . .Miss Casey." Her gaze swept over Patricia's clothes, and her expression tightened. She added coldly, "If Tim wants you to stay, of course you must, but I can take over his care now."

There was no mistaking the dismissal in the older woman's firm voice. Patricia stood her ground a moment longer, but then her head drooped and she turned and left the room.

Tim wanted to protest, but his head was worse. Other parts of his body felt battered as well. Exhaustion and pain were sweeping through him, blurring his thoughts even more. It was all he could do to swallow a few mouthfuls of the delicious soup Kate fed him. To his relief, it was far better than the broth his mother and then Kate had forced on him the few times he had been ill when a child.

He moved. Pain jolted through his leg as well as his head. His leg. It had been his leg that had bled so much, been infected. And he had fallen under that tree. No, no. . .Patricia had fallen out of the tree. On top of him.

"Are you sure Pat is all right?" he asked urgently. "She fell out of the tree."

"Pat?" Kate said forcefully, and then added in a hard voice, "So Jackie told us. Mrs. Wadding also informed us, amongst a lot of other stuff, that Miss Casey fell on top of you."

He peered up at her, disturbed by her tone. "Jackie? Good, he's back. But is Pat okay?"

She smiled at him and said in a quieter voice, "As far as I'm aware, that young lady is fine. Now, don't worry about anything. Just go back to sleep."

Tim was only too thankful to try and relax. He was glad Kate simply gave him a dose of medicine to dull the pain before telling him once more to get some sleep.

Tim obediently closed his eyes, but he couldn't rest. Anxiety swept through him. Kate was so cold toward Patricia.

Adam had glared furiously at both Pat and Andy.

And Adam had started to say something about Jackie.

He reached out and grabbed Kate's arm. "Don't let Adam do anything foolish about Pat and Andy until I've talked to him," he muttered urgently as he felt the medication start to take effect.

She was still for a moment.

"Please, Kate, my fault too," he managed to say.

She nodded abruptly. "All right, Tim. Now don't worry about anything except having that sleep."

&

"And I'm telling you, Mister, only a fool jumps a woman holding a gun on him. He's lucky I didn't shoot and ask questions later! He was asking to be shot, and a lot worse than he was."

Hearing her uncle's furious tones, Patricia caught her breath in dismay. She rushed into the large, well-stocked library and study where she and Tim had spent so many pleasant hours. A red-faced, furious Andy O'Donnell stood in front of an equally angry stranger who towered over him.

"I tell you it was his fault he made Patricia feel threatened enough to pull a gun on him to start with! What else was a frightened young woman—"

Guilt swept through Patricia. Andy broke off and both men stared at her as she hurried between them.

"Oh, Andy, pray do hush, you will disturb Tim."

"A little late for your solicitations, isn't it, Madam?"

"Andy!" Patricia grabbed her uncle's arm as he started to step around her.

"Why you. . .you. . .after all she's done!" Andy snarled. "Standing up to that quack, hardly a wink of sleep for days, nights. . ." He bit his lip tightly. At last, through gritted teeth he told Patricia "After all your sleepless nights and our care of that young rascal, this. . .this *gentleman* is talking about having you arrested for malicious injury!"

Patricia's hand tightened on Andy's arm for support as the blood drained from her head. Arrested? For hurting the man she loved, the man for whom she would die rather than see be hurt? If she went to prison, Danny might never be found. And her poor father. . .

As she stared dumbly at the stranger, the room started to tilt alarmingly. Vaguely she noted what fine clothes he was wearing. Mr. Stevens had said something to Tim about visitors. Important visitors by the looks of this one.

Someone moved forward. A lady's voice said quietly, "Now calm down, both of you. I'm sure there's no need to involve the police in any of this. John, can't you see the poor girl's exhausted? And from what we've been told, her fatigue is the result of her devoted care for Tim."

Patricia had managed to hide from Andy how badly shaken and bruised she herself had been from the fall out of the tree. Now, as she turned her head cautiously to stare at yet another stranger, the room continued to move alarmingly.

There was a wealth of compassion in this woman's kind eyes.

Whoever she was, the stranger was right. Patricia was exhausted. At first, sheer relief had swept through her when the capable Kate Stevens had arrived a couple of hours ago. Patricia had been so afraid there should have been something else they could have been doing for Tim. It would have been pointless sending to Bathurst for the doctor again after they had refused his choice of treatment for Tim the first time.

She had spent other sleepless nights caring for someone she loved, even her dear mother during the horrible time before her death. But this situation had been so different. Despite all her uncle's attempts at reassurance, she had felt the heavy responsibility of knowing she had caused Tim Hardy's injuries.

She—who had seen on the American frontier what guns could do, who always had hated guns—she, Patricia Casey, had shot someone. She had fallen out of a tree. Knocked Tim unconscious. She knew he had not fully recovered from the infected wound. Ever since they had carried Tim's unconscious body once more into the house, she'd felt that horrible, heartbreaking dread that he would never wake up.

Once more, the tears were not far away. But these tears were different. For days and nights, perhaps even years, these tears had been suppressed, never able to be released because it would mean she was no longer in control. Patricia fought desperately to hold them back. But she started to shake. The tears filled her eyes, rolled down her cheeks.

The tremendous strain had lasted for far too long. Her mother's death. Her brother being swallowed up by the army and the worry for his safety during the Mexican wars. Then he had been posted missing, believed killed. Andy had been lured off to the gold fields. Many of their cowboys had also gone. As her father slipped into depression, more work had fallen on her shoulders. Above all, only she had known the truth about Danny.

And through it all, that other horrible fear had ever been creeping closer. Talking to Tim and being reminded of some of her mother's teachings about God had been sweet, had held back that fear. Until she had fallen from that tree, for a few precious days she had even begun to wonder if God could possibly love her as her mother had always insisted—if the things Tim had talked about could be true.

But now, in her sorrow and exhaustion, the fear was back. Darker than ever.

God had deserted Patricia Casey.

He never answered her prayers.

Not once in all those dreadful hours trying to save her mother from her injuries. Not once through the years since Mother had died. Not once when Patricia had been unable to stop her brother and father from fighting so bitterly. Not when her brother had run away to the army.

For a little while she had hoped it had been God answering the desperate prayers wrenched from her that had saved Tim's life. But there had been no sense of God's presence. Deep down she knew Tim could quite easily have recovered without divine intervention.

Patricia Casey was all alone.

And now this.

The loving and caring God her mother and Tim's parents had believed in might be true for good people like them. But for some reason He had turned His back on the Casey family, on Patricia Casey especially. Despite her prayers over the years, there seemed no hope of help from Him.

She had caused injury to an innocent man, a good man, a man she loved with all her heart. When he had been unconscious again these last couple of days, she had been so frightened he was going to die. But even then she had found she could not pray. Patricia was quite convinced God had stopped listening to her prayers.

Surely He must hate her now.

And now Tim Hardy's employer and their friends all the way from England, rich and important people, were blaming her that Tim had come so close to losing his life. Tim had told her about Kate and Adam Stevens. And had the woman called this man John? Surely he couldn't be that old friend of Tim's father, the English lord he had spoken so fondly of?

Whoever they were, they loved Tim. They hated her.

And they were right to do so. She had nearly cost Tim Hardy his life. Twice.

The shaking grew worse. She moaned. A sob ripped from her. The tears flowed, a veritable torrent of them. The room began to whirl more violently. Vaguely she realized the big man called John was moving toward her. But next to her, Andy gave a cry of concern. She felt his arms go around her, supporting her as she fought to speak.

"I–I am so. . .so truly. . .sorry. I. . ."

That strange woman's voice cried out as the room spun even faster. Patricia crumpled.

eight

Tim woke slowly from a deep and dreamless sleep. Early morning sunlight was escaping into the room through the small space between the drawn curtains. He glanced swiftly around. No slight figure was curled into the comfortable armchair near the window.

Disappointment touched him. Only then did he realize how many times in his few conscious moments when his fever had been raging and more recently since he had hit his head he had been comforted by the small, red-haired woman's mere presence as well as by her capable hands.

His lips curled in a smile as he thought about her. Patricia. The most beautiful woman he had ever met, with her sun-kissed curls, her sparkling eyes. Who had made him angrier than he had ever been before with a woman. Who made him laugh with her wry sense of humor. Who made him stop and think about his relationship with Jesus Christ again. Who made him willing to think and even talk so freely about faith, about precious memories of his mother, his father. And there was still so much to tell her about his father, his last few puzzling words.

But Kate had tended to him since virtually chasing Patricia from the room. When he had last been awake sometime the previous evening, she had refused to allow him to see anyone or even talk, especially about Patricia or Andy. She had just fed him more soup, murmuring soothingly that all was well now that they were home. Before he could protest, she had quietly left the room, and as the pain in his head eased, sheer exhaustion had made him fall asleep.

Patricia. No doubt she was exhausted from looking after him day and night. He should be glad that she could rest and let Kate and Adam assume the work she had been doing. But he missed her.

Then he remembered the harsh words from Adam in this room. He frowned. That would have upset Patricia and no doubt roused Andy's quick temper.

Even though Adam and Kate were home, he wasn't so sure all was well. Adam had been furious, furious with Patricia and that gruff uncle of hers who had yet cared for Tim as gently as a father.

Why had Adam been so angry?

Mrs. Wadding. No doubt she had filled Kate's and Adam's ears with her spite. And hadn't someone mentioned Jackie?

A sense of urgency touched Tim.

He sat forward and moved his head cautiously. To his immense relief, his body's protest against the motion lasted briefly, encouraging him to swing his legs out of bed. The effort that simple action took surprised him. Perhaps he shouldn't attempt to walk unaided after all.

A small jug of water rested on the small table next to him. Eagerly he reached to remove the dainty throwover and pour himself a drink, but his hand was surprisingly shaky and he only succeeded in knocking over the jug.

Tim gave a loud, exasperated exclamation. As he grabbed at a small towel and tried to mop up the water spreading rapidly over the bedclothes, someone entered the room. Without looking up, he said in an irritated voice, "Do be careful where you walk, Kate. I'm afraid there's water everywhere. Sorry."

A man's voice replied with a trace of amusement, "Oh, I'm sure Kate won't mind in the least, young Tim. She'll be so relieved you are awake, and if I'm not mistaken, much improved."

Tim had abandoned his efforts as soon as the man started speaking. He stared at the very tall, well-built stranger standing just inside the room. Then he frowned. Surely he knew him, those dark blue eyes set beneath thick black eyebrows.

His voice, too, was familiar—that slight accent.

Amusement sparkled on the man's face, mingled with a trace of disappointment. "So, you don't remember me. Oh, well, it has been a long time, Tim lad. You were but a boy, and I have many gray hairs now and—"

"John. John Martin!"

Something flashed into the dark eyes, a hint of past pain.

Tim felt his face warm and added hurriedly, "Oh, Sir, I do beg your pardon. I–I meant Farnley. I did not mean to remind you. . . . Oh dear, I mean—"

He stopped abruptly and drew a deep breath. One hand raked through his tousled hair. With an effort, he pulled himself together and bowed his head formally. "Please accept my sincere apologies, my Lord Farnley. I fear the bump on my head has not only addled my brains but my good manners as well."

To his immense relief, John grinned at him. He advanced closer to the bed, saying cheerfully, "Well said, my dear boy."

That certainly was the old John Martin Tim remembered from when he was a boy, his father's first and dearest friend in this new land so many miles from their homeland.

John added quietly, "You were right the first time. John will do. It is such a relief to be away for awhile from being 'my lord this' and 'my lord that.' Oh, it is good to see you again, Tim."

Tim eagerly grasped John's proffered hand. But John did not stop there. His arms went around Tim and hugged him.

Tim's eyes grew moist. This man brought so many sad and sweet memories of Tim's mother and father. Not only had he once rescued Tim from a watery grave in the River Thames at great risk to his own life from his heavy convict's shackles, but he had also saved Tim's father's life on board the ship that had conveyed them both to their years of punishment in New South Wales.

John stood back and studied him. "And now it is my turn to apologize," he murmured a trifle ruefully. "You are certainly no longer the small, indomitable boy your father never could stop boasting about. From all I've heard about you, he would be even more proud of the man. And I am sorrier than ever now that this is the first time I have been back here in all these years."

Tim's throat tightened with emotion. "He. . .my father was most appreciative of the way you wrote to him, kept contact with him over the years since you. . .since you. . ." Tim hesitated, not sure if it was wise to remind this man of those dreadful years before he had been able to prove his innocence and his claim to be John Farnley, the rightful heir of his father's title and lands.

"Since I was able to throw off my convict clothes and put on robes suitable to wear before the queen?" John finished softly. He glanced down at his well-dressed person before looking thoughtfully back at Tim. "I can tell you it does not begin to compare to the sheer delight of being clothed in the righteousness of Christ so I can dare come into Almighty God's presence. And it was your dear father who led me to Jesus Christ."

Emotion made it nigh impossible for Tim to speak. In a similar, matter-of-fact way, his father had often mentioned aspects of his faith in Christ.

Tim swallowed rapidly and managed at last to say in a trembling voice, "You. . .you wrote that to my father once. He. . .he was so very happy that your faith was prevailing despite your change in circumstances."

Tim wondered just how the transition from convict to member of the privileged aristocracy had affected this man's faith. It would not have been easy to maintain the simple beliefs his father had espoused.

"And your faith, Tim? Has your trust in God prevailed despite all that has happened to you and those you love?"

Tim stiffened. He averted his gaze and moistened suddenly dry lips. Once again he was reminded of his father's directness when he was concerned about another's spiritual welfare. Suddenly Tim felt deeply ashamed. Would his father really be proud of the man he was now, a man who had let his child-hood faith wither so badly?

After a long pause, he looked up slowly. "It. . .it has taken a hammering, Sir."

John watched him keenly. There was no censure, only com-passion and understanding in his eyes. "Perhaps that is under-standable. I was so sorry to hear about your mother and little sister, and then for your father to. . ." He stopped.

Sadness filled John's eyes, and Tim looked away, afraid of his own emotions.

"And pray, my dear brother, what are you doing in here dis-turbing my patient?" Kate Stevens stood in the doorway. Mock indignation crossed her face as she surveyed them both.

John swung toward her and a smile chased away his grief. "Brother," he said slowly. "No matter how many times you call me that, you can have no idea how happy it makes me feel."

A slight blush rose in her cheeks, and she smiled back at him warmly. "We lived far too many years not knowing each other, my dear."

Tim looked at them a little curiously. So, even though John was now happily married to Elizabeth, even though he had children of his own, the man still took great delight in being acknowledged as Kate's brother. It made no difference they were really only half-brother and sister, they were still family. Of course, with his history, it was understandable that having a loving family was so all important to Lord John Farnley.

Once Tim had heard his mother and father discussing how horrible John Martin's upbringing in Spain must have been. From birth he had been wrongly taught that he was illegiti-mate, the son of an English soldier who had seduced his inno-cent Spanish mother. She had died in childbirth, and he had been reared by his Spanish relatives in an atmosphere of hate and hardship. Not until he reached adulthood and his bitter Spanish grandfather died was John Martin told the truth about his parents' true love and marriage.

Sadly, John's search for his father had led him to being the target of his malicious English cousin. That cousin had thought to prevent John being declared heir to what he had always considered his own heritage. It had not been until Adam Stevens had befriended John and with Kate's help proven his innocence that John had been set free to enjoy his inheritance and, more importantly, the wonder of his own loving family.

Now Tim no longer had a family. No matter how hard Adam and Kate had tried to make him part of their family, they had never been able to make up for the loss of the special bond he had enjoyed with his parents and for such a brief time with his small sister, Jane.

Kate moved closer and surveyed the wet bedding and the puddle of water spreading over the floor with a slight frown.

Tim fought back the old pain and managed to smile at her apologetically. "I'm sorry. Afraid I was rather clumsy."

She studied him carefully and then beamed. "Well, it seems you are much improved this morning. And this won't take long to clean up." She turned back to John. "Unfortunately the staff are in turmoil with our unexpected arrival, so, seeing you are here, John, you can help me get Tim up for a time while we change his sheets."

Tim stared at them. Certainly John was her brother, but to commandeer Lord Farnley's help like any servant. . .

Before Tim could voice his protest, John said cheerfully, "Most certainly, and perhaps I could help him bathe and shave as well. He'll feel more like his old self." He smiled at Tim's bemused face with a twinkle in his bright eyes. "Now, where might we find your dressing gown?"

Kate already had the garment in her hands, but as she placed it on the bed, Tim asked, "Patricia and Andy, are they still here?"

Kate and John looked at each other quickly.

"Adam hasn't sent them away, has he?" Tim asked in alarm.

"No, he didn't have to." John's voice was a trifle grim.

Tim stiffened. "Kate?"

"When we went to call them for breakfast this morning, they had gone. They must have sneaked away during the night," Kate said reluctantly. "No one claims to have seen them, although. . ." She frowned and added quickly, "They must have decided to continue their search for this Sean person they came all the way from America to find. But then we discovered—" She stopped abruptly, but Tim hardly noticed.

"Gone!" He was astonished at the depth of his dismay, the sense of loss. Something about Patricia Casey had stirred emotions he had not realized he had. She had seemed so strong, so independent, and yet vulnerable.

At Tim's dismayed exclamation, John said ruefully, "Yes, and it seems it might be my fault. My wife has forcefully told me that it is. I'm afraid I let that man Andy get under my skin, and I came on a bit too strong."

Kate snorted. "A bit too strong? You were talking about calling the police and having his niece arrested. Now," she added decisively, "they've gone, so let's forget about that pair and—"

"No, we can't forget about that pair," Tim burst out. "Pat saved my life."

John's dark eyebrows rose. "Pat?"

At the sudden speculative look his father's friend gave him, Tim felt heat touch his face. He looked steadily back at John and said carefully, "At first that's all she told me her name was." He hesitated for a moment, wondering just what Andy and his niece had said. "She wanted me to call her Patricia after she. . .afterward," he finished quickly.

"After she shot you, you mean?"

Tim looked quickly at Kate's stern face. "She told you about that?"

Kate shook her head. "Before we had alighted from the carriage, a very worried Jackie rushed over and told us you were unconscious once more. He had apparently arrived back here not long before us and received some hysterical story from the stupid housekeeper. For some—"

"The housekeeper? Is that woman still here?" Tim interrupted urgently.

"Why, yes," Kate replied abruptly. "We'll come to her in a minute. As I was saying, for some reason, Jackie was angry with himself, as though perhaps he could have prevented your being shot."

Kate searched his face. When Tim remained silent, she continued thoughtfully, "But then Jackie clammed up and wouldn't say another word, except that the doctor had been dismissed by Miss Casey despite Mrs. Wadding's strongest protests about your severe infection from a badly neglected bullet wound."

Tim frowned. "But I told you about my leg."

Kate nodded.

Jackie. Tim realized he owed the man a huge apology. And what must Jackie be thinking about Pat? Dear Pat.

Tim forced his thoughts back to Jackie and breathed a short sigh of relief that the aborigine had decided it best not to mention Tim's childish behavior. But Jackie certainly had no need to feel any guilt. Feeling confused, Tim stared from John to Kate.

John started to scowl and added briefly, "Miss Casey insisted she had shot you after her uncle at first tried to take the blame—if he is really her uncle. According to Mrs. Wadding, Miss Casey never calls him 'Uncle.'"

Tim gaped. That thought and its implications had not for one moment entered his mind. Suddenly he was angry with Lord John Farnley, with Kate Stevens, with all these adults who were failing to realize what a special person Patricia Casey was. Certainly she had tried to deceive him at first, but what else would a young woman do if confronted by a strange man when alone in the bush?

He thought of the indomitable girl who had not hesitated to draw a gun on him, the tender touch of her hands as she dressed his wound, the warmth of her smile while trying to hide the worry for him in her beautiful green eyes. A woman

who was so courageous and special she had reminded him of
Molly Hardy. A woman he had kissed. The one woman in the
whole world he longed to kiss again. To hold close. To never
let go.

Then he remembered the white-faced, exhausted woman he
had last seen standing up to Kate so steadfastly. That Patricia
Casey must have been very afraid to have run away in the
middle of the night. What had gone so horribly wrong?

Mrs. Wadding. She must have told her version of events to
them all, including Jackie. Tim should have sent her packing
when she had first started to disrupt the peace and harmony
of Waverley.

The growing anger in Tim exploded.

"If—of course he's her uncle! Whatever that. . .that horrible
woman may have told you," he said furiously. "And after all
they have done for me, you had no right to frighten them so
much they took off like that. They could have left me alone in
the bush if they had wanted to instead of bringing me safely
back to Waverley. Besides, it was an accident and as much my
fault as hers. Even Andy went for us both for being so stupid!
They are my friends, my very dear friends!"

John and Kate stared at Tim and then looked at each other.

"If you feel like that, then it's just as well Adam and Jackie
have chased after them, even if it was for retribution." Kate
stopped and then added swiftly, "We think they are probably
heading toward Sydney."

Relief flooded through Tim. Adam would find them.

"We are most annoyed with Jackie," Kate added abruptly,
her voice rising. "Apparently he saw them sneaking away just
before first light and did nothing to stop them. He did not say
a word about it to us until he realized we were anxious about
them. But why ever he thought we'd have given them—"

She stopped and bit her lip on the angry words.

Tim stared at her. She had used the word *retribution*. Alarm
swept through him. Something else was going on here.
"Given them? Given them what?" he snapped, looking from

one to the other.

Kate shrugged, avoiding Tim's gaze. "Oh, they helped themselves to some supplies." She glanced briefly at John and added firmly, "Now, let's get you up. I think you seem well enough to get dressed after all."

"Before I do, there is one thing I want you to promise to do," Tim said. As Kate looked at him he added angrily, "Send Mrs. Wadding packing, and don't let me catch a glimpse of her again."

Kate smiled slightly. "That is one thing that will give me great pleasure—if Adam hasn't already gotten rid of her. He couldn't stand her screeching."

As he submitted to John and Kate's help, Tim thought anxiously about Patricia and Andy. Even if they had helped themselves to supplies, he was relieved that at least they would have food to tide them over. And Adam was a compassionate man. With Jackie's help he would find the two Irish Americans, ensure Patricia and Andy were safe, and perhaps even coax them back to Waverley.

Another thought caused Tim to frown. "Did you say they wanted to find someone called Sean? Are you sure it wasn't a man called Danny?"

John replied, "I'm sure it was Sean—Sean McMurtrie."

Tim stared at him and then turned swiftly away, not wanting to raise any more doubts about Pat. Who was this man they had come so far to find? Was his real name Danny, or were there two men? Obviously their search was important to Pat and Andy since they had let it take them all the way to that isolated camp beside the Turon River.

Tim thought long and hard, trying to remember more of what they had talked about, especially before he had become so ill.

In all the hours they had spent together, why had Patricia never directly mentioned the man they were looking for? And what would this Sean, or Danny, be doing out there anyway?

Suddenly he doubted if Adam was right that they would go

back to Sydney, unless they had given up their search. Why would they give up now?

Tim drew in a swift breath as he remembered just where they had been camped, where they had been looking for that shepherd's hut. It had been a beautiful place, that creek meandering along the gully surrounded by those eucalyptus-covered hills with the flowering wattle dotted among them. Perhaps his father had thought so too. Perhaps that was why he had camped there. Perhaps. . .

Resolve settled on Tim. Whatever happened with Patricia and her uncle, he would return there. And soon. He was a man now, not a terrified fifteen year old.

It was time to put the past behind him.

nine

By the time Patricia and Andy had driven the few miles down the long road from the homestead to the high wooden archway denoting the entrance to Waverley Station, the sky in the east had lightened. Soon, weak sunlight would start peeping through the tall timber and scattered scrub on the rolling hills.

Patricia was hardly aware that Andy turned onto the main road heading toward Bathurst and Sydney instead of taking the rough track they had traveled with Tim. Her heart was sore. The last time she'd seen Waverley's neatly painted sign, she had been so thankful they had been able to follow Tim's mumbled directions, so thankful they could get help for him.

"You don't have to worry about Tim anymore," Andy said gruffly. He cleared his throat. "That young man certainly has plenty of help now and doesn't need you any longer."

That had been made only too clear when Kate Stevens had turned Patricia away from Tim's room. Pat shuddered as she thought of the scene that had preceded her faint. It had only lasted a few moments, and she had fought off all but Andy's strong arms. But she had not been able to resist the warmth and tender care of the woman she thought someone had called Elizabeth. Apparently, neither had Andy. Despite Patricia's protests that she could walk, he had carried her to her bedroom, placing her carefully on the bed. At first he had angrily resisted help from the woman who had followed them.

"Now, Sir, relative or not, you know it is not proper for you to be in Miss Casey's bedroom. I will help her," the woman had said very firmly. When he still didn't move, she had added more gently, "From what I have been told, she must be exhausted from caring for Tim. I'm sure she is only in need of a good sleep."

Feeling she could not take any more confrontation, Patricia had raised her head and whispered, "Please, Andy. I'll be fine. And you need rest too."

Andy had stared at her with narrowed eyes, then back at the woman holding the door for him to leave. He muttered something under his breath that made the woman's eyes flash, but to Patricia's relief he turned and left without another word.

Not even her own mother could have more tenderly wiped Patricia's tear-streaked face and helped her prepare for bed. She had been tucked in, even kissed gently on the forehead with a murmured, "God bless." Then the woman had said, "Try not to worry. The Lord is in control. Just sleep now."

Patricia must have fallen into an exhausted sleep almost before the woman had left the room. And Patricia still wasn't sure who she was—a friend of Tim? The wife of that angry man Andy had been arguing with?

Tim Hardy's friends obviously thought the world of him, were very protective of him. Patricia knew that Kate and Adam Stevens were the owners of Waverley and must have just returned from England. Patricia tensed and her eyes widened. John? Elizabeth? Could they possibly be the English aristocrats Tim had told her about? They had also come from England, and by the excitement of the old staff at Waverley, they were important and well known.

Patricia opened her mouth to ask Andy, but he had slowed the horse and was turning them into the bush.

"Andy, where are you. . . ?" The wheels jolted into a hole hidden in the deep shadows, and she hung onto the sides tightly to keep from being flung out of her seat. "Andy!"

He ignored her, peering ahead, steering the horse more carefully, deeper into the bush. She had to hold on as they were jolted from side to side. To her relief, after a few minutes, they jerked to a stop.

Andy handed the reins to her and muttered, "Won't be a moment." He jumped down, and she was still trying to steady the horse when Andy disappeared behind them.

The minutes passed, and Patricia became more agitated by Andy's absence. She was about to get out of the dray and tie up the horse to go looking for him when he appeared at last, breathing fast as though he had been running. Swiftly, he climbed up to sit beside her, and without a word, he took the reins once more.

"I was about to come looking for you," she said shortly.

He looked at her. For a moment she saw indecision in his eyes, but then he smiled crookedly and murmured, "Sure glad you didn't. Now, do you want your turn?"

She stared at him and felt the color rush into her face as she realized why he must have needed privacy. Folding her hands, she stared straight ahead and said primly, "No, thank you. I went to the outhouse before we left."

He grunted and shook the reins. The horse ambled forward once more, but after jolting along for a time, the bush became denser among tall gum trees. At last Andy gave a sigh, and they stopped.

"Guess I'm going to have to scout ahead for the best way," he muttered. "You'll have to drive. Think you can manage?"

Without waiting for her response, he handed the reins to Patricia and unhitched the saddled horse tied to the back of the dray. A weak beam of sunlight shone on the horse as Patricia turned to look. She gave a sharp exclamation.

"That's Blackie, Tim's horse!"

She had been in a deep sleep when Andy had woken her earlier that morning. It had still been dark, but he'd insisted they had to make an early start. "Never did stay a moment longer where I wasn't wanted," was all he'd said. She had been too sleepy to think clearly, too dazed and heavy hearted to protest.

Andy had their loaded dray waiting a little distance from the house, already harnessed to the big cart horse that had pulled it so faithfully all the way from Sydney. He had flung Patricia's few belongings in the back of the dray before swiftly tying the other horse to the back. Still in a daze of misery at leaving

Waverley, she had not even looked at the horse.

Now Andy ignored her cry until he was in the saddle, Blackie tossing his head and snorting. As Andy expertly gentled the horse, he said casually, "It's an exchange for our chestnut. It hasn't recovered from that sprained leg. And don't worry, I've been riding Blackie at Waverley for Tim."

Before she could question him further, he rode ahead, calling back over his shoulder, "Mind you, follow carefully now."

For a moment Patricia sat still. She had already noticed the extra bags of supplies in the back. The Stevenses had certainly been generous, but to let them have Blackie as well. . .

But then, she decided sadly, to lend the horse showed how anxious the Stevenses had been to have their guests depart, and Tim certainly would not be able to ride for some time. Even without the injury to his head and the bruises on his back and sides where she had landed on him, his almost-healed leg would make riding impossible for awhile.

Patricia sighed and urged the horse to follow Andy. As they continued on their way, the terrain became more rugged and hilly. She gritted her teeth, concentrating on controlling the horse. After awhile, they came out onto some kind of overgrown track, which was at least an improvement over forcing a new way through the bush. She was glad when Andy at last climbed back beside her and took over the driving.

It took a while for Patricia to realize they were no longer heading toward Bathurst, but instead followed a northeast route. It might be the track they had followed with Tim, but she was too tired to care much anymore. At least this change meant that Andy had decided to try to follow the last lead they had been given about Danny.

She'd never seen Andy so grim faced. When they stopped at long last to rest and water the horses, he thrust a water bottle at her, followed by some bread and cheese. Patricia was thirsty, but after only a few mouthfuls of food, she could eat no more.

Andy, too, looked exhausted. His face was pale and strained.

But he insisted they move on after only the briefest stop.

Patricia had started to take for granted they were going back to where Tim had stumbled over them, but after awhile Andy swung west. She thought of protesting, of telling him about the gold dust she had panned. But what did finding a few grains of gold, if it were gold, really matter anymore?

Even as she hesitated, Andy broke his long silence, saying quietly, "I promised to help you find Danny, Pat, but this has to be our last attempt to track him down. We'll make discreet enquiries in the village at Orange, even go on farther west to that place called Wellington. If there are no more leads for a red-haired, heavily freckled man with an accent similar to our own and calling himself Sean McMurtrie, then we return to Sydney and take the first ship back home."

Although his voice was low, his decisive tones and stern demeanor kept her from arguing. Tears filled her eyes. She brushed them angrily aside. In her heart she had already said good-bye to Tim Hardy.

"Patricia?"

Andy's voice had sharpened. Rarely did he ever call her by her full name when they were alone. She nodded, not able to trust her voice. He was silent, but after a moment she heard him give a deep sigh before slapping the reins to urge the horse to a trot.

They crossed a few dry creek beds and then managed to find a crossing over a much wider river that fortunately had knee-deep water. It was very rough in many places. Sometimes Andy climbed onto Blackie to try to find a better way through the steep gullies for the dray. Several times they had to backtrack and try a different route.

Patricia didn't dare question the tight-lipped Andy O'Donnell. A measure of his tension was the two guns he wore for the first time since they'd arrived at Waverley. It saddened her to see them. They seemed to change Andy in a way she did not like.

Throughout the day, she had thought about the threat made

to have them arrested. Andy had confirmed that the man who had made the threat was indeed Lord Farnley, but Patricia was not terribly worried about the matter. She trusted Tim to put it right. He had always said the gunshot was an accident and had even teased her about it until he had seen how upset the reminder of it made her. But then again, Andy had always claimed with an Irishman's conviction that one could never trust the English aristocracy.

Patricia had never seen her uncle quite like this, so angry, so grim. And she was still weary, sad at leaving Waverley without a word of farewell, even though Andy had assured her he had done and said all that was necessary. The thought that he could not possibly have said all to Tim Hardy that she wanted to had been forced back to the secret place deep within her where so much other sorrow was stored.

It seemed like the well of grief just kept getting fuller, deeper. Her mother. Her father. Danny disappearing the way he had. The change in Andy. And now Tim Hardy.

Patricia sat up a little straighter. Her lips settled in a tight, firm line. Those moments with Tim, that kiss, and her dreams had been a fantasy. There could be no future for the son of an English convict living in Australia and the daughter of Irish immigrants living in America.

She tried to brush the thoughts away, to concentrate on guiding the horse so he would not break a leg or tip the dray over on the uneven ground. But thoughts of the young man with the twinkling warm amber eyes who had strolled toward her across the sand on the Turon River, who had kissed her so tenderly with love and passion in his eyes would not be easily dismissed.

And Patricia had plenty of time for thinking. Their progress was slow, much too slow for Andy, who refused to stop until the sun had set. She could tell he was on edge as he carefully chose a sheltered place to set up camp. But he was very gentle with her, insisting she rest while he looked after the horses and prepared a meal. She was glad to let him do so, although he must have been more exhausted than she was.

Once again, she forced some food past her lips—food that had not required a fire, she noted with some surprise. But it was a passing thought, gone long before they had finished their brief meal. Swaying with exhaustion, she obediently crawled under the dray and onto the pile of bedding Andy had prepared for her. As was his custom, he would bed down a little distance away. In a few moments she was sound asleep.

When Andy shook Patricia awake, faint light in the eastern sky was just beginning to disperse the darkness. He already had the horses ready but looked as though he had not slept much, if at all.

That night they again camped in thick bush. Andy let Patricia clear a safe area and gather sufficient wood to light a fire long enough to heat water for a hot drink, but he insisted on dousing it as the evening shadows deepened. She nearly rebelled, longing for a hot water wash rather than the cold water he pulled from a creek for her. But he turned away from her glare so decisively that she remained silent. Had something happened at Waverley that he had not told her about?

Still feeling the effects of the sleepless nights and days caring for Tim, as well as the exhausting days of travel, Patricia fell asleep while still thinking about it all. But some hours later she awoke. Light from the full moon showed Andy sound asleep a little distance from her. Something moved just beyond him. It was a measure of how deeply Andy slept that he did not stir when a couple kangaroos hopped into the small circle of moonlight not far from him.

Patricia was enthralled. Several times, especially in the evening or early morning, she had seen the strange animals moving swiftly through the bush, but she had never seen them so close before. The kangaroos straightened, resting on their strong back legs and long, thick tails. Standing perfectly still, only their ears twitched back, forward, to the sides. Something moved on the nearest animal. To Patricia's delight a tiny head peeped out into the moonlight from its mother's pouch.

One of the two horses tethered a little distance away moved, jingling the hobbles. The kangaroos took flight, crashing their way through the bush.

Andy was on his feet in a flash. To Patricia's dismay, she saw the glint of moonlight on the rifle in his hands as he swung it up, glaring around him.

For a moment she could not move, but then she lowered her head cautiously, not once taking her eyes from her uncle. As far as she knew, Andy had never slept with his rifle beside him, at least not here in Australia. Something was definitely wrong to make him so on edge.

A moment later, he lowered the rifle. He muttered something and stared toward her. Suddenly he seemed menacing, not at all like the uncle who in recent months had been like a father to her.

She dared not move, thankful she was in the dark shadows under the trees. Hopefully he could not see her. She tried to shake off the feeling, to call out to him, but then she heard him swear softly, viciously, before returning to his bedding.

Andy never swore. At least not in her presence. Stunned, she slowly lay down and stared up at the starry sky. Had he simply reacted instinctively to being woken from a sound sleep? Yet the more she thought about the last few days, the more she realized Andy was acting as though they were under a threat of some kind.

Until now, she had been too weary and depressed to think clearly about their departure from Waverley. But her senses were wide awake at last. Frantically, she examined what had happened from the moment Andy had woken her that night.

So they did not disturb anyone, he had insisted she move quietly as they packed her few things and crept from the house. There had been that moment when one of the horses had snorted as they approached. Andy had tensed and then hurried her even faster. It seemed now as though they had been sneaking away from Waverley, not wanting anyone to know they were leaving.

They had only traveled that very short distance on the main road before turning back into the bush. While she had been waiting for him, had Andy gone to erase any sign of where they had turned off? If he thought someone might be following them, he would do just that. He had shown her many such tricks over the years—ways to hide a trail he had learned from the Indians and experienced frontier men. And he had been a little too cautious about where they camped, each morning obliterating as many signs of their camping as possible.

How foolish and blind she had been. They were running away. Hiding.

Why? Had Lord Farnley or Adam Stevens really sent for the police? What had been said after she had gone to her room?

She thought about Kate Stevens and the woman called Elizabeth. She dared not let herself think about Tim. Certainly the men had been angry and upset enough, but Andy knew Tim would put things right. And if Andy were really afraid of her being arrested, why were they going so close to Orange? Did he think the only police in the area were at Bathurst?

When they had been making enquiries about Danny at an inn on the road near Bathurst, Andy had left her to watch the horses while he went inside. She had started chatting to a friendly old man. He had proudly told her he came from Orange, explaining that it had been called Blackman's Swamp until just four years back.

"Called after a bloke named John Blackman," the old man had said, grinning at her from around the pipe dangling from his lips. "Not them pesky blackfellas that ran rampart here with their fierce tribal wars. Our Blackman became chief constable at Bathurst. But the name did confuse some." He chuckled. "Might be the real reason we're called Orange, although the official reason is it's on account of the explorer Mitchell, what discovered this neck of the woods, worked for that there Prince of Orange or somethin'."

Patricia had smiled back, wanting to ask more about the

aborigines but listening patiently as the man continued his rambling history lesson. It had only been four years since the plan for the village had been approved by the government. The first sale of surveyed allotments had been held less than two years before. The first public building had been a watch house, the Methodists had erected a small brick building, there had been several slab huts built, but not much land had been sold, he had informed her a trifle gloomily.

A watch house. That meant there was a police presence in Orange. Suddenly Patricia wondered if she had ever mentioned that to Andy—as she still had not mentioned the gold dust hidden among her few clothes.

She bit her lip and shrugged. After all, it was only a small amount of gold. But would Andy think that, or would that feverish glint come into his eyes as she had seen it in California before he had taken off to the gold fields? That look had been in her brother's eyes, too, and even in her heartbroken father's eyes the last time she'd seen him. Perhaps Andy had a right to know, to decide if they should go back to the Turon River to search for the precious metal while they were here.

There was little sleep for Patricia the rest of the night. She was up and dressed long before Andy stirred in the chilly morning. She watched him as he rose and stretched. He stilled when he noticed she had lit the fire and steam was starting to rise from the water heating over it.

"I thought I told you not to light a fire," he said angrily, heading toward the fire.

She moved swiftly to stand in front of him. "And why would that be, Andy O'Donnell?"

He stopped.

"Afraid someone might be chasing after us?"

They stared at each other. Andy studied her defiant face and at last nodded. "That, too, but more because it has been too dry and we wouldn't like to start one of those bush fires we've been warned about, would we now?"

Patricia felt uncertain. She looked around. They had

camped close to the trees. The undergrowth certainly was very dry. "We could have camped beside that creek farther back," she said sharply.

Andy shrugged and then sighed. "Yes, we could have. And then we would also have been easier to find."

She closed her eyes and whispered hoarsely, "We are really hiding. They sent someone to the authorities?"

Andy was silent, and her eyelids flew open. He looked uncertain. "I don't know for sure," he admitted defensively, but then added bitterly, his Irish accent suddenly very strong, "but you saw how that English lord fellow was attacking us. Our people learned a long time ago not to trust the English, especially their aristocrats!"

"Our people," she whispered. "You. . .you mean the Irish?"

"Yes, the Irish," he roared. "Your own flesh and blood. Your own grandfather transported, here to this very colony, falsely betrayed by an English lord who pretended to be his friend while plotting to take his land, our home. My. . .my father. . ." His voice cracked. He turned away but not before she saw the anguish on his face.

Patricia dimly remembered overhearing her mother once saying something to her brother about forgiving those who had disrupted their family. But Andy had bitterly retorted that it was very well for her to talk about forgiveness; it had all happened when she was too small to remember. Patricia knew her grandfather had died when her mother was very small, her grandmother soon afterward. The two children had been reared by a distant relative. But there her mother had always stopped, leaving Patricia to guess at their difficult life, which Andy had eventually escaped after his sister had been safely married. Obviously Andy had been old enough to remember.

Andy stood with his back to her, his shoulders hunched slightly. She moved swiftly and stood behind him, putting her hand gently on his shoulder.

"I'm sorry, Andy," she murmured. "Ma. . .Ma never talked much about anyone in her family but you, and then just that you were reared by relatives until you migrated to America."

He turned swiftly and tugged her into his arms. "And you are all I have left of family now," he said fiercely. "I'll do anything to protect you."

Not until then had Patricia ever appreciated the love this man held for her. She hugged him back and said earnestly, "I know you will, Andy dear. I love you, and I am so privileged, so thankful to have you look out for me, help me. But. . ." She drew a deep breath and let him go. Taking a step back, she added gently, "But I am an adult now. Don't you think you should have told me we were running away?"

"I didn't think you were in any fit state," he said harshly. "You scared the life out of me when you fainted. But even before that I could see how fond you were getting of that young fella."

Her eyes widened. She opened her mouth, but he waved his hand and added impatiently, "Oh, I know you didn't realize it yourself at first. I wanted to get you away before you did, even before those people arrived back home. What hope could there ever be of a future for you with someone like Tim Hardy, especially when you have your home so far away?"

His words only expressed what Patricia had been trying to convince herself of. She looked away.

"Then, before they had so much as met us," Andy continued, indignation and anger making his voice rise again, "they believed that nonsense Jackie and then Mrs. Wadding filled their heads with. That. . .that Lord Farnley was so furious! He was going to have you arrested, even though his wife was so nice to you afterward."

Patricia stared at him doubtfully. "But. . .but Lady Farnley was lovely to me. Said 'God bless' to me. Assured me that He had everything in control. She. . .she even kissed me."

Andy's eyes widened in surprise and then narrowed.

"Andy, you were too angry to think straight. Probably more angry at being confronted by an English lord than anything else." His eyes flashed fire, but she added swiftly, "I am sure

they are decent and fair people. Tim told me the Stevenses—
the Farnleys, too, for that matter—are very strong Christians.
It is obvious how much they all love Tim. And remember, he
told us he was only the son of a convict. Lady Farnley did not
have to put me to bed herself. Would most English aristocrats,
at least like you have known, do that to a stranger rather than
order a servant to do so?"

He looked uncertain, and she continued relentlessly. "I
think you are wrong, Andy. These people are different; they
care. I am sure she at least would not have let the police be
involved, especially after we looked after Tim so well.
Besides, as soon as he could, Tim would tell them what really
happened."

Patricia took a deep breath and then said pleadingly, "I
think we should go back to Waverley and try to put things
right."

Andy's face paled. He opened his mouth, closed it again,
and swallowed. He looked from her across to where Blackie
was searching for some green shoots in the dry grass.
Patricia's heart plunged even farther.

"This last day I've known I–I had the temper on me for
sure." Andy swallowed again. "We can't go back," he whispered hoarsely, "because now they would certainly arrest us,
but for thieving, perhaps even horse theft."

"Blackie?" She stared at him with increasing horror. "You. . .
you stole Blackie?"

For a moment Andy did not move. Then he nodded, flash-
ing her one swift glance before looking away. "I lost me temper," he muttered again, and she saw the shame that filled him
at what he had let his temper do.

Patricia swayed. They may have been entitled to help themselves to some provisions until they had reached a town
where they could buy their own, but this. . .

They had stolen Tim Hardy's horse! Tim loved that horse.
He had told her many stories about Blackie as a colt, about
adventures they had shared together. Even if Tim could have

forgiven her all the physical suffering she had caused, there was no excuse for stealing his horse.

That knowledge was bad enough. But it was the other thought that came racing through her mind, that made a low moan slip from her lips. *Tim Hardy will most surely hate me now.*

❧

"I am not a horse thief!" Andy roared, punctuating each word by slapping a clenched fist against his other hand.

Patricia looked up at him for a long moment. "If that is so, then it is time the horse you borrowed was returned," she said for what seemed the hundredth time. "Unfortunately the food we have eaten is another matter. Perhaps we could send some payment for it."

He looked away, staring off through the trees at the culti-vated paddock that informed them Orange township was not far away. She did not stir, returning her gaze to the defiantly blazing campfire and the vegetables cooking on it, not even glancing up when at last he stomped away.

They had been arguing ever since he'd told her about Blackie. Now the sun was high in the sky, but she had refused point blank to move one step until Andy promised to return Blackie to Waverley.

At first, she'd wanted to simply turn around and go back. Although deep down she believed the people at Waverley would never do so, she had reluctantly accepted the possibil-ity that they just might have Andy, at least, arrested. Besides, he had adamantly declared there was no way he would go back near that English lord. She had just as stubbornly in-sisted that the least they could do was return Tim's horse.

A snort from Blackie and a shuffle of sound made her look over her shoulder. She sprang to her feet. Andy was swinging up into the saddle. He stared at her, his lips in a tight, angry line. As she opened her mouth, he pulled on the reins and kicked the horse into motion.

"Andy," she called, but Blackie broke into a brisk trot and

Andy was gone in the direction of the Orange village.

Relief mixed with trepidation. Was he going for supplies and information about Danny as he had originally planned, or would he return Blackie? She looked at the solid but slow old cart horse and bit her lip. Should she follow him? She could not leave all their belongings here. It would mean driving the horse and dray by herself into town and then hoping to find Andy.

Reluctantly she decided it would be best to stay put. She would serve them both well by allowing Andy time alone so his anger could fade.

"But you could have at least let me give you a note of apology to post," she muttered and then moved slowly to douse the fire and wait anxiously for Andy to return.

Then a horrible thought struck her. She had not warned Andy about the watch house at Orange or of the possible law enforcement officers who might be there.

ten

Tim stared from the grim-faced Adam Stevens to the scowling John Farnley. "What do you mean, there's no sign of them? Couldn't Jackie track them?"

It was the third day since Patricia and her uncle had disappeared. Adam had just returned alone from Bathurst. He tossed his dusty, wide-brimmed hat on the floor of the verandah beside Tim's chair and wearily sank down onto an old canvas chair. Staring out across the dry paddocks toward the distant, tree-covered line of hills, he said curtly, "We didn't try to track them at first. We went too quickly, hoping to catch up with them before they reached Bathurst. Had not been there long when Jackie went all native, as he can. Rattled off a few aboriginal words or, when I got really annoyed with him, stared from that expressionless face of his without a word."

John quietly asked, "What happened to upset him this time?"

Adam scowled. "The usual, I'm afraid. But for some reason ever since we arrived home, he's seemed upset with Tim as much as with himself for letting Tim get sick." He fixed Tim with a glare. "You wouldn't like to tell me why, I suppose?"

Tim hesitated, knowing how wrong he had been to use Jackie in that crazy way. To his shame he knew it had been a childish attempt to impress a beautiful woman. A woman who had just humiliated him by shooting him!

Now that same Patricia Casey's absence from his life left him feeling as though some vital part of him were missing. As wonderful as it had been to get to know John and Elizabeth as an adult and having Kate treat him like a son, Tim found himself listening for that lilting Irish accent, waiting for her brisk step, missing her saucy smile, her compassionate eyes.

Kate and Elizabeth joined them in a whirl of petticoats,

114

forcing his attention back to the issue at hand. He swallowed, glad that the interruption caused by their arrival with a servant carrying a tray of refreshments made any response to Adam's question unnecessary.

Tim ignored Kate's frown when he waved away the cup of tea offered to him. Adam fell on his with relish, and Tim had to wait until he had swallowed several mouthfuls before prompting him to finish telling them what had happened.

Adam studied him long enough for Tim to begin feeling not much older than the young lad his father had left with them all those years ago. But he wasn't that same person anymore. He was a man, and it was time his old friend and mentor recognized that.

Tim raised his chin and stared back at Adam steadily.

Elizabeth came to his rescue. "Do tell us what happened. You said you saw or heard nothing of our young friend and her uncle?" she asked eagerly.

"Friend!" Adam snorted.

His wife interjected smoothly, "Yes. After what Tim has told us, we are most decided that Miss Casey and Mr. O'Donnell are indeed our friends. Despite what we have been told, their care of Tim has made that very evident. They dismissed that Dr. Mint not only because he wanted to bleed Tim, but because he wanted to amputate his foot! Oh, and by the way, I have sent that Mrs. Wadding packing. Tim had actually dismissed her just before he hurt his head."

Husband and wife exchanged a look that Tim had noticed many times over the years. Kate's head was raised, her eyes steady on Adam's. Whatever he saw in her face made Adam relax suddenly and smile so sweetly at her that a pang of envy whipped through Tim. Her smile in return was full of the understanding and love they shared for each other.

John muttered dryly, "And as their 'friends,' I have been told we should do all we can to help them."

"But of course," Elizabeth said matter-of-factly and sipped at her tea. "It is what Jesus would want us to do."

Adam suddenly gave a low chuckle. "So be it then."

A wave of love for these people swept through Tim. He and his family owed so much to them. Kate and Adam had always maintained they owed his father much more for the faith in God he had demonstrated and taught them. Yet their trust in God, their love for Him seemed to grow each year. Yet Tim knew their stories, knew that even in recent years they had suffered loss and disappointments. Life had not been easy for Elizabeth and John either. The stigma of John once being a convict still clung to them in England.

Shame hit Tim hard as he admitted to himself how he had allowed his own faith to shrivel in comparison to theirs. These four friends had learned to forgive, to leave the past in the hands of their loving heavenly Father. They were totally committed to living out their lives in a way honoring to Him.

Tim's heart swelled. Their change in attitude toward Patricia Casey and Andy O'Donnell was so typical of them, so typical of the way his own father and mother would have behaved.

So many times, he had been told the stories of his father's part in their coming to faith. Such had been the strength of his witness, that he had brought John to faith. Then by the Christian life they had demonstrated, together they had won Adam to trust Jesus Christ. Elizabeth and Kate, too, had grown from having a shallow religious faith to experiencing a deep personal relationship with God in Christ.

All had not become smooth sailing after that. Only a couple years ago Tim had watched Adam and Kate grieve over the loss of a baby. He had seen their tears, their anguish. Until then, in his immaturity, he had thought Christians were not supposed to grieve as he had at the death of his father. He learned through watching Adam and Kate that grief was natural and tears brought God's gift of healing.

Unlike Tim, the Stevenses had not let their terrible time of sadness separate them from God. Instead they had let the experience draw them closer to Him and to each other. Their trust in a loving and merciful God had never wavered. Their voyage back to England had been undertaken to help the whole family during their time of grief.

And I have ruined their homecoming.

"Perhaps we had best forget about Patricia Casey and Adam O'Donnell," Tim said in a harsh voice.

Four pairs of eyes stared at him.

"They said they were here trying to find a man called Danny, or Sean something or other, so we should just let them get on about their business," he muttered.

"But they have made their business ours by what they did to you and for you," Kate commented quietly.

"I did it to myself by intruding on them in the first place!"

They were silent, the two couples exchanging glances.

"But you were so adamant we find them," John said gently, "and given the way they looked after you, I do believe we owe them at least the peace of mind that we intend them no harm." He paused and then added stiffly, "And I am afraid I did not behave at all as Christ would have me do when I lost my temper. That alone needs to be put right."

Tim stared at him and then at the others. Kate and Adam slowly nodded in agreement. Elizabeth smiled approvingly at her husband.

"We, too, were at fault," Kate murmured with regret.

Adam began to frown thoughtfully. "Sean, did you say, Tim? Do you remember the man's other name?"

Tim thought hard but at last shook his head. Despite all the hours they had spent together, except for that one time she had blurted out they had to find someone, Pat had always changed the subject when their conversations had swung to why she and Andy were in Australia. Not for the first time, Tim thought it strange that she had never talked about this person they wanted to find, never asked him if he had any knowledge of the man. Surely after they had become such good friends these past weeks she could have mentioned him!

Or had they only been friends from his perspective? he

wondered a little bitterly. Perhaps that kiss had meant nothing to her. She had told him stories about an older brother, but Tim could not recall her mentioning his name. This man could be a brother, but he could just as easily be her husband, a lover. . .

Pain lashed Tim's heart. Patricia's reticence was simple. She had not trusted him enough to tell him.

"I actually met a man at the inn in Bathurst called Sean," Adam said quietly. "Sean McMurtrie it was. I noticed him first because he had an accent so similar to that girl. Even looked like her. I introduced myself and mentioned he looked very like a young woman called Patricia Casey I had recently met on my station and was looking for. He seemed startled but then laughed it off and hastily left, claiming he had an urgent appointment to keep."

"He looked like her!" Tim's heart suddenly lightened. Then he scowled. But her brother would have the same name, Casey.

Watching Tim closely, Adam said, "Yes, he looked very much like her."

"Then that settles it," Elizabeth exclaimed with a happy laugh. "We have to find them and, if for no other reason—" she paused and smiled lovingly at her husband, "—make sure they know the man may be still in the district. For them to travel all the way from America to find him, he must be very important to them."

Tim shut his eyes against the burning behind them, annoyed that his physical weakness still made it so hard to control his emotions. The love these people were demonstrating was overwhelming. To help someone else, no matter who they were or what they had done was as natural as breathing to these four. All because "Jesus would do so." A consuming desire filled him to have a similar relationship with God.

Kate stood up and began gathering their afternoon tea. "Right, gentlemen," she said brightly, "Elizabeth and I will see about a meal while you talk strategies."

Adam and John laughed out loud at her. "And then you two will come and tell us what you have decided," John said in a teasing voice.

The women looked at each other a shade ruefully before smiling back at them and retreating into the house.

The men were silent until John said quietly, "So if Patricia Casey and Andy O'Donnell were so keen to find this Sean McMurtrie, the only conclusions we can reach are that you missed them in Bathurst or they never went there at all. They may have gone north to where they were searching before. We need Jackie. Do you have any idea when he might condescend to return home?"

Adam shrugged. "Jackie took offense at something one of the aboriginal half-caste servants at the inn said to him. It must have been the last straw. That's when he went into his old routine of not speaking any English. The next morning he just drawled that he was 'goin' walkabout, Boss' and rode off. If you want to find them—or get Blackie back for that matter—that leaves us with the alternative of informing the authorities and—"

"No way," Tim interjected. "I've already told John if you report them to the police I'll deny everything. The bullet wound was my fault, and I gave Andy permission to ride my horse."

Adam looked at Tim with surprise. John's scowl deepened for a moment, but then that thoughtful, knowing look spread over his face.

"Let me finish," Adam responded. "I only mean we may need help to find them, not arrest them."

Feeling a little foolish, Tim turned hastily away but not before he saw the twinkle dawn in John's eyes as it had several times during the last few days whenever there had been any mention of Patricia or her uncle. He suddenly realized how much he had talked about her. The heat started to climb into his face.

He avoided looking at John as Adam continued calmly, "I

didn't mean to tell the police any more than that we need to find them to give them an urgent message. I was going to add, perhaps we might be able to find that Sean McMurtrie for them. He may have some idea where they could be."

Tim started up out of his chair. He grabbed the crude wooden crutch John had fashioned for him.

"It's certainly good to see you up and about, Tim," Adam added smoothly, "but do take it easy. I can tell that Kate is still worried about you and—"

"And he's improving rapidly each day. He's surprised everyone by the way he is so rapidly regaining his strength," John interrupted, "especially if his temper is anything to go by when the women start fussing over him too much." He grinned cheerfully at Tim.

Tim felt the heat rise to his cheeks once more. Several times his anxiety about Patricia and Andy had made him grouchy, short tempered. He had not been able to bear thinking of the possibility of never seeing Patricia again.

Before Tim could defend himself, John added meaningfully, "Adam, I think it's about time you and Kate realized that Timothy Hardy's beloved son is a man in his own right and not a boy to be mollycoddled."

Tim stared at John gratefully. He straightened. "Thank you, John," he said crisply, "and I would be most grateful if there is no more talk of police in this whole business. Andy is not a bad man. He is just very protective of his niece."

Tim remembered the look in the Irishman's eyes over the barrels of those two guns. Too protective? To the extent of harming anyone who threatened her with harm?

Then Tim remembered the soothing voice that had calmed him when he was feverish, the tender way Andy had helped his niece care for him. He added firmly, "We'll wait a few days and see if Jackie returns or sends us a message. By then I should be much stronger."

He saw alarm flash into Adam's face. Before the man could object, Tim added swiftly, "I'll decide what we will do after we hear from Jackie. In the meantime, I'm sure neither Patricia nor Andy will harm Blackie. They must have had a good reason for what they did, but when they realize a warrant has not been issued for their arrest, my guess is they will eventually return Blackie or at least let us know where he is."

He saw the doubt in both faces but was relieved when John and Adam nodded slowly in agreement.

Tim turned and awkwardly started to make his way inside, trying to ignore the throb in his leg and head that reminded him he would have to be patient for some time before. . .

He drew in a deep breath and stopped. Before he found the one woman he loved and longed to spend his life with.

Impulsively he swung around. Adam was still watching him, a slightly puzzled frown on his face. John was staring intently across the paddocks and the road to the house.

"It's only fair you both know." Tim drew himself up and said quietly, steadily, "Patricia Casey is the first young woman to ever remind me of my mother's indomitable spirit and loving heart. I intend to ask her to marry me and would be extremely happy if she could find her way clear to have me."

A picture of Patricia flashed straight to his heart, blotting out the surprise and then frown on Adam's face. Oh, how he wanted once more to see her beautiful lips start to curl into a smile that then reached her incredible green eyes, to light those eyes with mischief, with sparkling laughter, with that other fleeting expression he had never quite been able to understand. A sharp longing to find Pat so he could bathe in her beauty and warmth flashed through him.

"Tim," Adam began hesitantly, "you don't need my permission, but are you sure that—"

"Gentlemen," John exclaimed as he stood to his feet, "we have visitors."

Something in his voice brought Adam to his feet as well.

Two horseman had just passed the tall gum tree lookout and had kicked their horses into a trot down the last slope to the homestead. The younger of the two men increased his lead on the other. His large hat bounced behind his head, revealing a face and fiery red hair that brought Tim swiftly forward.

As the stranger pulled his horse to a stop, he glared up at them with an urgent, grim expression.

Even before the man opened his mouth, Tim knew it was more imperative than ever that they find Pat and her uncle without delay.

⠀⠀⠀⠀⠀⠀⠀⠀⠀⠀⠀⠀⠀ ❧

It was dark before Patricia heard a horse approaching. She grabbed the rifle Andy had left behind and slipped into the shadows away from the light of the fire.

"Patricia?"

She breathed a sigh of relief at the sound of Andy's voice and moved swiftly toward him. He rode into the light and dismounted from a chestnut horse.

"Thank you, Andy," she said softly. "Did you have any trouble?"

"No," he said shortly, "but I thought it safer to stable Blackie and send a note to Waverley for someone to collect him."

He started attending to the horse, finally leading it off to hobble and tether near the other one. She had expected him to still be angry with her and was not surprised when he did not speak to her until after he had eaten the food she silently dished up for him.

Speaking formally, he said, "Patricia, I have a terrible temper on me. I am really sorry I let it get out of control so that I have shamed you like a common criminal. Would you please accept my sincere apologies?"

She flew toward him and knelt at his side. "Oh, of course I do."

For a moment she felt the tension in his body as she put her arms tightly around him. She knew only too well what it was to have a temper. She also knew what an effort it had been for this proud man to humble himself by apologizing.

"I love you, Uncle Andy," she murmured and kissed his bristly cheek.

She felt his body relax, and then he hugged her back. "You haven't called me that for a long time," he murmured in a choked voice.

"Haven't I? How remiss of me, but it was you who forbade it. Said it made you feel too old," she whispered, tears choking her own voice. Giving him another hug, she sat back and said anxiously, "Did you hear any word about Danny?"

She didn't need to see the shake of his head to know the answer. If he'd had news, Andy would have been excited and told her immediately.

Andy sighed. "So, we go on to Wellington first thing in the morning. I didn't see any police, but there is a watch house in Orange. We must avoid the main road and follow the Bell River to its junction with the Macquarie at Wellington. The Turon also runs into the Macquarie." After a pause, he added softly, "You do realize this is our last chance?"

She nodded sadly. Only a miracle would help them find Danny.

That night, unable to sleep, she knelt on her blanket, and despite her fears that God did not listen to her, she prayed fervently for a miracle. Then she was still. At last, with tears streaming down her face, she whispered repeatedly, "I'm sorry, God, so very, very sorry."

In the cold light of day, she wondered why she had bothered. She didn't feel any different. Even if she had been wrong before, this last escapade must surely have turned God against her. There would be no miracles for Patricia Casey.

❧

Some of the country Andy and Patricia traversed over the next few days was even more steep and rugged, slowing their progress significantly. Then one evening when they had just come over a ridge, they started down a steep slope and were suddenly in the midst of a small flock of sheep. The animals dodged off in all directions. Two disgruntled shepherds shouted and then started after the scattered flock. Immediately Andy handed the reins to Patricia and jumped down to help.

At first the two men were very abrupt, but after Andy had helped round up the sheep, he successfully used his apologies and Irish charm to good effect. The two shepherds greeted Patricia politely, if a little warily. The one who had introduced himself as Billy seemed friendly enough, perhaps a shade too friendly. He smiled smoothly and professed himself very glad to see anyone so pretty to help relieve the monotony of droving sheep with only sheep dogs for company.

The other man studied her without speaking. She wished she could see his eyes, but his wide-brimmed hat was pulled low on his forehead. At last he nodded and in a cold, quiet voice said, "Ma'am."

Patricia was taken aback by the shepherds' rough, filthy clothes, their unshaven faces, and the coarse language. She wasn't sure what to think when Andy, hesitating only briefly, accepted their offer to share their campfire. While they shared some of their food with the two men, she remained quiet, listening to the men talk. Andy was adroit at parrying any curiosity about their own affairs while at the same time drawing the men out about their business.

Billy told them cheerfully that the station they had come from was so short of feed from the long stretch of dry weather that they were trying to fatten the sheep along the riverbank before taking them to markets at Wellington in a few weeks.

Although the quiet man his friend called Harry left most of the talking to Billy, it soon became apparent Harry was the leader. Patricia appreciated the fact that, unlike Billy, Harry at least removed his hat and washed his hands before eating. But as the evening wore on, she decided he was watching her too much. He seemed fascinated with her red curls. At first she only felt uncomfortable, but he kept staring at them until she began to feel a little belligerent. Always she had been self-conscious of her hair coloring, especially since she had cut it unfashionably short for this journey.

She stared back at Harry crossly, ready to tell him to stop being so rude, but he looked away and muttered, "Never seen hair quite like that before, and then two in a couple of weeks."

Patricia drew in a sharp breath. Andy swung around.

Before either could speak, the other drover, busy tidying away the remains of their meal, chuckled. "Reckon it looks much better on her than the young bloke, though. He had a lot of freckles too."

Patricia sat stunned. Before she or Andy could ask about Danny or mention his name, Harry drawled thoughtfully, "McMurtrie not only had hair like yours, but his accent was just like yours, too, I reckon, Miss." He stopped suddenly and peered at her intently. "Now, like him, would you be originally from old Ireland, Miss?"

Before she could speak, Andy laughed. "Not for many years, I'm afraid."

The garrulous drover scratched his head and said slowly, "That bloke were a strange one. Said he'd heard talk of gold being found in this area and was askin' us about it."

He eyed Patricia and Andy keenly before adding, "Reckoned he'd been in some place in America where he had worked on the gold fields in California near where the rush started a year or so back. Claimed to have overheard some big Australian bloke boastin' that in the Bathurst area was the same kinda of rocks they was diggin' up and findin' gold in. He said he thought the bloke's name was Hargraves, but we'd never heard of him."

Patricia opened her mouth and then snapped it shut as Andy interjected, "Well, guess it would be like one of them fairy tales come true for a young bloke to find gold out here."

He stood up, stretched, and yawned as though not the least interested in the red-haired man or any stories about gold in Australia. His Irish brogue was even broader as he added casually, "Not sure what I'd be doin' with a lot of gold though. A bit might be nice, but too much would be bringin' too many problems, I'm thinkin'. Now, it's been a long haul today. Guess it's time we got some sleep."

Patricia stared at Andy, incensed at his not questioning the men further. He shot her a warning glance. When she turned back to the men, she realized Harry was watching them intently. He stared at her, and for a moment the strange look in his eyes perturbed her. But then he smiled slightly, and she thought it must have just been the light from the campfire playing tricks.

"Yeah," Harry said softly, "I suppose it would be like a fairy tale—but a nice one at that. A man could do a lot of things, go a lot of places with money," he added wistfully. "But still. . ." He shrugged. "There've been tales over the last twenty to thirty years of gold being found in Australia from the mountains south even to here, but there's been no gold rush here like that bloke told us about where he come from."

Patricia stared at Harry, not liking the expression in his dark eyes one bit.

The drover's lips moved in a brief smile that did not reach those eyes. "I reckon there's a heap of gold waiting to be found right here by some lucky bloke. Why, only a few years ago someone in England wrote an article claiming he'd seen samples of gold from here and predicting that gold would be found in great quantities in Australia," the man murmured, still watching her.

Abruptly, Patricia turned away. Despite Harry's rough appearance, he was no ordinary working man. And he certainly seemed interested in gold. As in California, the sparsely populated areas of New South Wales would contain men from all walks of life. Some would be simply trying out a different lifestyle, some trying to get a new start, but some would be trying to escape something in their past.

She winced and glanced at her uncle. She was sure that not only Danny was one of that latter group, but so also was Andy O'Donnell.

Harry was still speaking thoughtfully, his gaze on the fire that was gradually dying down. The shadows deepened on their faces. "Some think the governor then was scared of what effect a gold rush might have. There's rumors that over ten years back Sir George Gipps refused to let stories of gold finds made then be given publicity. But I knew old McGregor and know for a fact the rumors about him were true."

"McGregor?"

Harry glanced up at Patricia and Andy before looking away and adding slowly, "He was a shepherd working on a property near Wellington. Found gold not far from here a few years back. He's probably out there somewhere now trying to find more."

Harry laughed grimly and glanced up at Andy again, who was frowning. "Guess Gipps was right. Everyone would leave their humdrum lives and rush off to find gold and perhaps the everyday running of the country might come to a halt. But a lot of blokes have gone and joined the search in America anyway, so the powers that be are offering a reward for finding worthwhile gold in Australia."

Billy laughed. "And wouldn't you just love to find some of that lovely yellow stuff, Mate! You're always talking about going off to California. But perhaps you won't have to go that far with the rumors around here more recently. That young Sean fella sure pricked up his ears at your story of that bloke called Smith who's recently been claiming he's found gold. Won't say exactly where of course, but rumors say he was prospectin' east of Orange. When we told him, he lit outa here real fast. Reckon he's already over there somewhere tryin' his luck."

Harry grunted and stood up. He scattered the hot coals and then busied himself pouring water on the fire, making sure every spark was out.

Andy shook his head ever so slightly at Patricia. She swallowed the words hot on her tongue and also stood, giving a forced laugh. "And I suppose you gentlemen egged him on in his foolishness. Oh, well, I'm to bed too. Good night, everyone."

But excitement kept her awake long into the night. She had to tell Andy about the gold.

The next morning, Andy was very quiet. He looked tired, as though he, too, had not slept well. She found out why after they had waved good-bye to their hosts.

"I'm not sure I trust those fellows, especially that quiet one," Andy said abruptly. "I decided seeing it was going to be dark in a few minutes, it would be best to camp with them than risk having them creep up on us."

Her eyes widened. "You stayed awake all night, didn't you?"

He nodded grimly.

"But you do think that was Danny they met?"

He nodded again. "I don't suppose there'd be too many men out here answering his description and with an accent like ours."

To Patricia's relief, Andy added wearily, "Looks like we go back southeast of here to where we were before at the Turon. That's twice we've heard he could be in that area. Let's just hope Danny hasn't left by now and is back in Sydney."

eleven

The wattle trees lining the steep gully on the other side of the narrow Turon River were drooping in the heat of the afternoon. When she and Andy had first visited this place, Patricia had been enchanted by the golden balls of fluff that had so liberally covered the trees. Now only a few brown reminders of that splendor lay on the ground beneath the silver-leafed trees. But other bushes were starting to flower in the early summer heat. Wildflowers struggled to survive along the banks of the river as they competed with the native grasses for moisture.

Not once had it rained since they had left the Blue Mountains. Tim had mentioned that it had been unusually dry. Waverley needed rain so that its pastures would be green for the sheep and cattle, not to mention its acres of wheat that needed moisture for a good harvest.

Tim.

No matter how she tried to banish him from her mind, he kept invading her thoughts. Today especially, Patricia had been inundated with memories of Tim Hardy's quiet, deep tones telling her about that day his father had died near this very place, how she had held him to her, comforted him.

And now there was the cave and what she had just found in it.

Shivering, she forced her eyes away from the old landslide of rocks and dirt that she had scrambled over to reach the cave. Filling the camp water container first, she then scooped up water in her tin mug. She drank deeply of the cool, refreshing liquid, refilled the mug, and started back up the steep bank to the shade of a large old gum tree. She wiped perspiration from her face and eagerly drank more.

The days were becoming hotter. In the two days since she and Andy had set up camp here, the water level had dropped noticeably. And this was only late spring. By December it would be much worse.

Patricia looked thoughtfully down at the creek bed. Perhaps God had brought them back to this very river where she had met Tim Hardy for a purpose. The idea had crossed her mind several times that day. Mary Casey would have thought so for she had always claimed not to believe in coincidences, only in God's leading. Especially if one prayed for Him to lead!

Patricia sighed. The bittersweet memory of her mother's faith died away, and the old ache flowed through her. Certainly she had reached rock bottom that night at Waverley. There was no doubt her thoughts and fears had been exaggerated then by sheer exhaustion and despair. But still, she had prayed for God to lead her more than once these last few years, these last few days especially, and until now she had thought her prayers were a waste of time.

Her prayers recently had been sheer acts of desperation. Deep down, she wondered if God didn't want to listen to her prayers, let alone answer them.

Yet Tim so obviously believed in prayer.

Well, for that matter so did she. It was just Patricia Casey's prayers she doubted God listened to.

She had prayed for Tim with all her heart that dreadful night when they had battled so hard to get his roaring fever down. He had certainly recovered.

But had God really heard her prayer, or would Tim have recovered anyway? And then, Patricia had prayed for a miracle to find Danny. Would God use rough men like those drovers? They were nothing like what she had always thought angels might be!

"Oh, God, if You are listening, if You do care what happens, could You please, please tell me what to do now?"

The prayer burst from her. Her loud words startled a magpie just above her and it took off in a flutter of wings. Once more there was only the soft sounds of the breeze through the bush and the burble of the creek. Patricia leaned forward, clasped her hands around her battered trousers, and rested her head on her knees.

After a long moment she stirred and sighed wearily. There had been no blinding flash of wisdom, no sense of what she should do. And as for Tim Hardy. . .

She had tried so hard to push that young man into her past with all her other heartbreaks. But he refused to stay there.

Irritated with herself, Patricia took another long swallow of water. So many times she had promised herself she would not think of Tim, but it had been impossible, especially since they had set up camp on this stretch of the Turon.

And now this.

She still had not told Andy about the gold dust hidden among her possessions. Until they had returned here, the discovery had lost any importance to her. Yet somehow, they had come right back here to where she had found the gold.

Andy had left early again that morning, muttering something about hoping to find the shepherd's hut they had been told was somewhere in this vicinity. Each day, as soon as the sound of his horse's hoofbeats faded away, Patricia had not been able to resist panning for more gold. Until today, only a small amount had been added to her hoard, but this morning there had been more, much more.

In California that gold would have been worth many dollars, and it had been found in only a relatively few hours with her small pan. If she could find more gold, she could pay Andy something for this whole journey to Australia.

Each time the color of gold had shown in the bottom of her pan that morning, excitement had flown through her in waves. She had found herself feverishly washing more and more pans of dirt, knowing that many gold prospectors would have been incredibly excited at finding half as much gold as she had in such a short space of time. It might be that the whole area, the banks and hills, were well worth prospecting.

Then she had stilled. Why, she was no different from those men filled with gold fever, the men she had been so critical of. Suddenly ashamed, she had returned her pan, small spade, and the gold to camp. Then she had set out, determined to climb up the cliff to the cave still waiting to be explored. Andy had pointed it out the day they had set up camp. Neither of them had noticed it before, even though it was some way past where that cross still clung to the gum tree. Andy thought a fresh fall of rocks and earth might have revealed it.

Now, Patricia not only had to wonder what to do about her gold discovery but also about what she had discovered in the cave.

Again she wondered, had God been leading all along? She remembered Tim once saying something about "God working things out for good for those who loved Him."

It could certainly not have been God who had caused her to shoot Tim. That was clearly her own stupidity. But had God led them here for reasons other than simply finding Danny? The more she thought about it, the more bewildered she felt. How could it all possibly tie together?

Patricia made herself more comfortable against the trunk of the gnarled old gum tree and closed her eyes. She wondered if those drovers had finished taking their sheep to the property back out west they had claimed to come from. She frowned. There had been something about them, especially that quiet one, that had made her feel uneasy even before Andy had expressed his reservations. Had it just been their talk of gold?

Patricia shook her head. It had been a more personal wariness, a womanly one.

She wondered if, after listening to their stories, Andy had wanted to search for gold around here even more than he'd wanted to look for Danny. Perhaps the way Andy's eyes had gleamed at the talk of gold had been the real reason she had not yet told him about her find. She had seen what fever the thought of finding gold could bring to the sanest of men. Even her own stern father.

She shivered again. Now she knew what that gold fever felt like. Would she have reacted so crazily to Tim Hardy if she had not just found that gold? Would Tim Hardy get that same feverish look in his eyes at the thought of finding his own gold, of becoming rich?

With a sigh, Patricia tried once more to banish Tim from her mind, concentrating on thoughts of Danny. He should be her chief concern, not a man who had been a complete stranger only a few weeks ago.

And yet, she thought wistfully, *after only those first few days he seemed someone I could know so well.*

Tim had been so sweet worrying about causing her too much trouble, and yet so strong in the way he had coped with pain and illness.

Danny. She had to think of Danny.

She had never told Tim that Danny was her brother. Regret flooded through her. Would she ever have the chance to now?

She frowned, forcing her thoughts back to her brother. Surely if Danny had been in this area prospecting for gold, they would have come across him by now. Her heart had sunk a little farther each day as Andy became more taciturn. She was surprised he had not insisted they return to Sydney long before this. Perhaps he would have if he still did not believe that Lord Farnley and his friends would have the police waiting for them.

But even Patricia's hope was fading fast. There simply was no sign of Danny. For days, she'd seen no sign of any living thing except the creatures of the wild. And this river basin, this whole country was so vast. The way they had picked up Danny's trail as soon as they had gotten off the ship in Sydney had been a miracle.

Miracles.

Had meeting those drovers been one of God's miracles? Her lips twisted wryly at the thought of those men being anyone's idea of a miracle. Her smile faded fast. The thought would not be banished. Was God helping them? Leading them?

"Are You, God?" she murmured. "Are You leading us as Ma said You would? Perhaps You know how desperately I need to find Danny. But You knew how desperately I wanted Ma to live, how desperately I want Pa to love me. Danny is all I have left. Are You even now leading Andy to find him?"

Wearily she moistened one corner of her filthy shirt with water and swiped it over her hot, sweaty face. It still seemed strange that in late November the days were becoming hotter instead of colder. Back home in the northern hemisphere, the trees in the mountains near their ranch would have almost finished carpeting the ground with their yellow and golden leaves. The animals in the wild would be energetically stocking up food and preparing for winter.

Patricia wondered sadly how her father was coping. Had he returned home? He had abruptly told her one day that he had decided to try his luck for awhile on the gold fields. The very next day he had packed up and left with little more than a muttered farewell. With a heavy heart at the change in her father, she had stood and watched until he was out of sight, only then allowing the tears to flow.

Then Andy had arrived and inevitably dragged out the whole story about Danny, how instead of being killed he was a deserter and had begged her not to tell their father. Several weeks before, she had received a letter from him telling her he was going to Australia to search for gold and a new life.

Many times since then she had wondered if her father had returned and found her note or had ever bothered to write to her. Had he found any gold?

A wry smile twisted her lips. As she had?

He certainly hadn't written to her before she and Andy had left the ranch. Probably Michael Casey never missed his daughter. Patricia swallowed, feeling the burn of tears prick her eyes.

She scrambled to her feet, picked up the water, and turned toward the track leading to their campsite set well back from the river. She set her shoulders. Already she had decided that when she and Andy returned home, with or without Danny, she would make her father listen to her, talk to her.

She stilled. The sound of movement came from downstream.

Andy had expected to be away for hours. Of course, it could be cattle, even kangaroos. Yet. . .

The sound grew nearer. Hoofbeats clattered swiftly over the stones and sand beside the running water.

And she had left the rifle back at camp.

Ever since meeting the drovers, Andy had insisted she always have the rifle near at hand even though she resolutely refused to wear the revolver. She hated guns even more now but had obeyed Andy. If there were other men in the bush like those drovers. . . All day she had kept the rifle with her, but it had been too heavy to carry with the water barrel.

There was no time to make it to camp for the gun now. She looked around. Only a few tall gum trees stood nearby, little vegetation to hide in.

A horse snorted. She heard the swift click of hooves on the large, smooth rock not far from the outcropping she could see.

Patricia dived for a small bush, peering anxiously toward the bend in the river. A few moments later she breathed a sigh of relief as Andy came into view on the chestnut horse. She stood up and started scrambling down the slope toward him. As he rounded the bend, he kicked the horse into a sudden gallop along the straight stretch of sand past the track leading up to their camp. She opened her mouth to call out to him, when he saw her. Frantically he waved her back, gesturing with a finger to his lips for her to be quiet.

He pulled on the reins, but only slowed the horse to a walk as he drew level with her. "Get out of sight," he commanded harshly in a voice that barely reached her. "Someone's following me." He urged the horse on toward the next bend in the river.

Patricia's heart leaped. Her thoughts flew to Tim. Had he guessed where to find them? There had never been any real doubt in her mind that Andy was wrong. Tim would never let the police be sent after them.

She hesitated.

As Andy disappeared, the clatter of more horses sounded on the rocks he had just crossed. Then Patricia made out the sound of voices.

Her heart thumping, she scrambled back up the track. She had almost reached the shelter of the bush when a voice called out. For a moment she thought it had called her name.

Could it possibly be Tim?

She twisted her head to look, stumbled on a rock, and fell sideways. The earth moved beneath her. An involuntary cry escaped, even as she felt the ground give way completely. Then she fell in a tumble of dirt and rocks, desperately trying to grab hold of anything to stop her descent.

Something hit her head.

She stopped fighting and let the tide take her where it would.

Someone was swearing. Another harsh voice said, "Quiet, you! She's not hurt much. Help me to get her out of sight. This is a golden opportunity."

Not sure if she had passed out for awhile or not, Patricia groaned as she felt someone grab her under the shoulders and start dragging her. Some relief came when other hands lifted her legs and her body left the ground. After a few minutes she was dumped down. Pain knifed through her back, her head. She groaned again.

"Get some water," that same harsh voice commanded.

"I ain't goin' back down there," another voice protested. "He'll be back. Won't let this little girlie far out of his sight. We'd better get out of here. He knows we're followin' him now anyways."

Patricia forced her eyes open. Dazed, she stared up into a face she recognized only too well. It was furious. Fear swept in fast as the anger on the bearded face changed to that look that made her flesh creep.

"What. . .what are you doing here?" she gasped.

Bold eyes swept over her disheveled body. She shrank back and started to push herself up, but her head spun too much.

"Why, Miss Casey, we were just riding along, minding our own business, when you fell down right at our feet," the drover Harry smirked. Then hardness swept over his unshaven face. "And now you can help us find it."

"Find. . .find what?" She put a hand to where her head was stinging. It felt damp.

"The gold, of course."

He knew about the gold!

She lifted her eyes to his face. He was watching her intently. As she stared at him in astonishment, a faint gleam of excitement changed his expression.

He nodded slowly. "So I was right. You have been stashing gold away. Looks like we've found what we were looking for, Billy lad!" he added triumphantly.

Again Patricia tried to lever herself up but fell back with a low moan. She felt as though her body had. . .had fallen down the riverbank.

"Go get a drink for the little lady, Billy, and then she just might show her appreciation of your kindness by telling us where it is. Reckon we might even get our dray and set up camp here nice and close to the river."

Billy protested once more, but after a brief argument and a few more sharp words from Harry, the man disappeared. Patricia looked around her. They had carried her some distance back from the river into the thick bush not that far from where their camp was hidden.

She stared at the drover, the quiet one she had not liked at all. He was looking at her body in that way she feared and hated. And she was alone with him.

Trying hard not to let her voice shake, she said haltingly, "We. . .we haven't been stashing gold away."

"No? Then what is all that bright stuff that man of yours has been getting out of the river? He should have a nice pile now, surely enough for us to go and claim that reward from the government."

Andy had been finding gold? Shock held her still. All those days they had been here, he had been panning the river too? What about searching for Danny? Her heart sank. Perhaps he had given that up after all.

Harry grabbed her fiercely by the arm. Then he reached out his other hand and ran a filthy finger down her cheek and then her neck. She cringed, frightened even more by his scorching eyes.

"Reckon I might have some fun making you tell us at that," he muttered, then licked his lips.

"And I reckon not," a soft, deadly voice said from behind him.

Patricia gave a sob of thankfulness.

The drover grabbed for the rifle near his feet.

"No," Andy's voice whipped out. "I wouldn't touch that if you want to live."

The drover froze and stared at the two revolvers pointed at him. Andy had stepped from behind an old river gum.

"Get away from him, Patricia."

She obediently crawled a few feet away before starting to get to her feet. Dizziness swept through her, and she sank back to the ground. "I. . .hit my head," she gasped. "Be right in a moment."

"You've hurt her! I ought to shoot you right now!" Andy snarled in such ferocious tones, he even scared Patricia.

"No, no," she called out, "the riverbank gave way under me." She made another effort and this time regained her feet. "He. . .he said you had found gold, and he wanted me to tell them where you had hidden it."

Andy gave a mirthless laugh. "So I was right. Someone has been watching me the last few days."

"The last few days?" the drover snarled. "We only arrived this morning."

"We? There's more of you?"

Andy went on full alert, but he was too late. Patricia screamed, but the piece of wood in Billy's hand did its work.

Andy's finger hit the trigger, and one of his revolvers went off. The bullet plowed uselessly into the ground as he went sprawling.

And then lay horribly still.

twelve

"Andy!"

Patricia started toward him, but Billy reached him first, and Harry grabbed her by the arms. She struggled, but he was too big, too strong. She had wrenched her shoulder as well, and her struggles only made the pain worse. Harry flung her to the ground. Pain knifed through her, and she went limp.

When she came to, she was lying on the ground, her head resting on Andy's lap. He was sitting propped against a tree. One large hand was smoothing her hair, but both his hands were tied. She groaned.

Relief echoed in his voice as he whispered, "Hush now, me darlin'. Just rest quiet for a few more minutes. Be worse than you really are—or I hope you are."

Worse than she was? A sharp pain knifed through her head. Every inch felt bruised and battered. Then she understood. Her ankles were tied, but her hands were free. She obediently closed her eyes.

Another voice snarled, "We ain't got more time to let 'er wake up properly. You tell us where that gold is, and then she can rest."

"Billy, Billy, where are your manners?" Harry's cold, quiet voice admonished mockingly. "Let's give the little lady a bit more time. Perhaps that drink? I'm sure very soon we can persuade them to tell us all," he added menacingly.

Patricia felt Andy tense. A hand roughly shook her shoulder. The moan that whelmed up in her was no fake. She opened her eyes. A cup was thrust into her hands. She almost dropped it, but Andy's hands were there.

"Can't you see she's hurt bad?" he snarled.

Billy hesitated but after a moment stomped back to his

140

comrade. "Reckon you're right," he snarled. "She's still too crook—"

"Crook? You're the crooks," Andy snarled.

They both stared at him. For a moment they looked affronted, but then Billy began to chuckle. "Reckon we've just taught this bloke another Australian meaning to that word. Crook means sick, you idiot!"

His companion was not appeased. "Hmm, perhaps if we hurt her more, make her even more *crook,* her man will talk."

Andy stiffened and only relaxed slightly when Billy said vehemently, "I ain't hurtin' no woman, and neither are you."

Harry gave a low, laughing sneer.

"Have a drink, Darlin'," Andy said loudly, and then he added under his breath, "but make it like you're still out of it. Might get a chance to untie me."

He coaxed her until she managed to sip a few mouthfuls. She didn't have to pretend very much at first, but she did peer around as her head slowly stopped spinning. They were still in the small clearing surrounded by thick bush. The men were talking quietly around a campfire several feet away, and a small dray was a little distance away from them.

She looked up anxiously at Andy. A bruise and some scrapes marked his pale face where he must have hit the ground. "Are you hurt much?" she whispered.

He shook his head slightly. "And you?" he asked in a soft, tight voice. "Did they hurt you?"

"No, no," she said softly, and something in his eyes relaxed. "That track gave way. I have a few bumps and bruises. Except for my head, I should be fine. How long have we been here?"

Andy shrugged. "I don't know," he muttered with relief in his voice. His gaze returned to the two drovers. "When I came to, they had tied me up and already had a fire going. Must be a little while."

"What. . .what are we going to do, Andy?"

He shrugged, his eyes on their captors. "Get away somehow. Lie down again. Pretend to be sick, asleep."

She gave a realistic groan and rested her head back on his knee so her face was hidden from the other men. Her trembling fingers started working on the rope around Andy's wrists.

She whispered, "Is there really any gold stashed away, Andy?"

He stiffened. She glanced up. His lips were twisted slightly, but his eyes had darkened. "Quite a bit more than you have in that bandanna of yours," he admitted quietly.

She gasped.

"I found it when I was looking for more bandages for Tim and remembered you had been washing dirt here." He paused. A puzzled look with a touch of hurt flashed into his eyes. "Why didn't you tell me?"

"I. . .I don't know," she faltered. "I had just found it when Tim arrived that first day. That's the main reason I was so jumpy. Later, he was sick and. . ." She put her hands on his. "I–I guess I just forgot it for awhile and then—"

"Forgot!" He looked at her with amused affection. "So like your mother. Only someone like Mary could forget finding gold!"

"Hey, what you two doin'?" a voice asked threateningly.

Patricia froze. The men were walking toward them. Too late, she closed her eyes. Andy's ropes were tied so tightly, she had made no progress.

"Now, don't you go gettin' any ideas of untyin' him, Missy, or I'll have to tie you up too!"

"Oh, I don't think tying her up yet is an option. We'll just separate them," Harry said in a cold voice, so calm and matter of fact that Patricia felt suddenly very afraid. He added, "I think Miss Casey will be more than happy to behave once I've finished with her tonight."

"You touch her, and I'll kill you." Andy's voice was low and deadly.

"No, you won't," a familiar voice said furiously from behind them. "I'll reserve that pleasure for myself."

Patricia gasped and cried out, "Danny! Oh, Danny!"

Harry and Billy dove for their weapons. Two rifles thundered, kicking up dirt near their feet. They froze as three other men stepped from the shelter of the bush, surrounding them. A dark-skinned man also slipped from the deepening shadows, a long spear balanced, ready to throw. The other three men had their guns aimed at the two drovers. One was a weathered, gray-haired man whose rifle had roared at the same time Danny had fired. The other two Pat recognized as Lord Farnley and Adam Stevens.

A deep voice from behind Patricia said calmly, "Good shooting. But I think that will be enough for now."

Patricia started and peered up at the two men behind her. "Danny? Is that really you?" she whispered. "And. . .and Tim?" she said incredulously as her gaze shifted to the man standing beside Danny.

He hurriedly tossed his rifle down and crouched beside her. "Pat, have they hurt you?" he asked in a strained voice.

She stared at Tim, then turned her head once more toward Danny, and then to where the two drovers were being forced to lie on the ground. He was still there, that gray-haired man. He was helping Lord Farnley pull the two drovers' hands behind their backs, starting to tie them up. She shut her eyes tightly and opened them again, sure that the figure would have vanished. *But he was still there.*

Andy was also staring across the clearing. He gave a short, incredulous bark of laughter. "Well, I don't believe it!"

Gentle hands touched Patricia's shoulders, turning her around. She stared up at Tim, seeing the fear in his eyes. Danny had already cut the ropes on her ankles and was busy attending to Andy's.

"Pat, oh my darling Pat, you must be all right." The urgency in Tim's voice increased. "There's blood on your head, your hands," he croaked.

She kept staring at him. Everything was happening too fast.

Tim ran his hands gently over her arms, her legs. "Where are you hurt?"

The touch of near panic in Tim's voice reached her at last. Still hardly daring to believe, she leaned forward. With a choked exclamation, Tim caught her in his arms and pillowed her against his chest.

"Careful there," Danny warned, "that's my sister you're touching."

Patricia didn't stir. Not even for Danny. She felt safety as she had never known before in Tim's tender embrace.

Someone gently pushed aside her dirty, blood-caked hair and lifted her head from its warm resting place. Someone touched the back of her head. She groaned and put her face back on its comfortable pillow.

"Careful, Man," a cool voice said. "She must have hit her head. Can't see much else wrong with her though except scratches."

She forced her eyes open. That horrible Lord Farnley was frowning at her.

"Oh, thank You, God!" Tim's dear familiar voice held a world of relief.

Patricia looked straight into his concerned amber eyes. The arms cradling her tightened. She closed her eyes. It must all be a mistake. She must have hit her head harder than she thought.

Another voice asked anxiously, "Are you hurt anywhere else, Patty? Those men. . .did they harm you?"

She opened her eyes and swiftly turned her head at the same time. Not a good idea. Pain slashed through her, and she fought back a groan.

The question had come from the gray-haired man who had been with Lord Farnley and Adam Stevens across the clearing. She gazed up at him, still wondering if she was dreaming. His lips smiled gently, lovingly at her in a way she had not seen for far too long.

"Pa?" she whispered.

Tears sparkled in his faded eyes. He crouched down. A gnarled hand reached out and touched her face as gently as a feather.

"Yeah, it's your stupid old pa at last."

It was. It really was. Relief, elation swept through her. And he was with Danny!

Her father cleared his throat. "I didn't stay on the gold fields," he confessed. "Must have just missed you by a couple of days. Besides your note, a letter was waiting." He swallowed and added gruffly, "Went straight off to see about a pardon for this idiot before hightailin' it to Bathurst. Deserting from the army, making you promise not to tell even me! Some stupid idea you both had I might be so noble as to turn in my own son!"

"No, no," Danny protested swiftly, "I–I was more ashamed of you thinking me a coward than that."

"You wrote to Pa!"

Danny hesitated. He twisted his hat in his hands and ran his fingers through the head of red curls so like her own. "Wasn't fair to let him think I was dead," he muttered, "especially once I was relatively safe here."

"And didn't I try and tell you that over and over?" she said with a flash of temper. She tried to scramble to her feet, but Tim's arms prevented her.

Tim had been angry for days, but that anger intensified at what he perceived as thoughtless neglect of the woman he loved. Glaring at Patricia's father and brother, he barked, "Can't this all wait? Pat's been through a nasty ordeal."

Tim's anger at the two men had started the day they had ridden into Waverley, having followed Adam from Bathurst. Apparently after Adam had spoken to "Sean McMurtrie" in Bathurst, Danny had told his father, and they had followed Adam. "We guessed it could only have been that wonderful, protective sister of mine and Andy who the guy was looking for," Danny had explained gruffly. Only after they were reassured that no harm was intended to Patricia or Andy had Danny and Michael Casey been persuaded to tell their own story and then allowed to join the search party.

"Surely you can sort this all out when we've seen to your

injuries, Pat," Tim now said in a carefully controlled voice. "Just stay where you are until we make sure. . . ." He faltered, at last losing the little self-control he had left. All he had been feeling over the past few days consumed him. In a strangled voice, he cried out desperately, "Pat, Darling, you frightened the life out of me!"

Tim cleared his throat. "I'll never to my dying day forget how I felt when Jackie appeared out of the bush with his tale of what he had seen happen to you. Then we heard a distant gunshot. I knew Andy must be somewhere, but it could have been your captors shooting and. . . Oh, I am so thankful to God that He brought us right here!"

Was that a glimpse of joy he'd detected in Pat's eyes when he first spoke? Now, of all things, unmistakable concern followed swiftly by anger darkened her face.

"Whatever are you doing here anyway, Tim Hardy? You are as white as a sheet. You shouldn't even be riding a horse yet! Your injuries. . .let me go!"

Tim gaped at her. Instead of letting her go, his grasp tightened. She had fallen, injured herself, been taken captive and tied up, just been reunited with her father and brother, and she was worried about *him?*

John Farnley started to smile. "I know what you mean about dear Molly Hardy now," he murmured to Tim.

Tim glanced up. Michael and Danny Casey were scowling, staring at John suspiciously. Although John had already made significant cracks in their prejudices, obviously it would take more than a few days for the two Irishmen to overcome their natural aversion and mistrust of an English lord.

Dismissing them all from his thoughts, Tim turned back to Patricia. He was oblivious to everything except the wonderful woman whose small, capable hands pushed at his arms, forcing him to let her go. Patricia stood up and swayed.

He reached for her again, but she groaned, "Don't touch me. Where's Andy?"

John gave a snort of laughter.

As Tim disobediently slipped an arm around Patricia to steady her, he glared at the man.

John swiftly turned his laugh into a cough, explaining, "Your uncle is fine. Adam's just tending to his injuries."

"Where *is* Andy? We've got to tell you. . ." Patricia's voice weakened. "So much to tell you, Tim, but Andy, he has to agree to. . ." She swayed.

Tim saw a look of sadness and regret touch the face of Michael Casey as his daughter searched for Andy. Tim glanced from John's curious expression back to the mild shock and indecision still on both Danny and Michael Casey's faces as they watched Patricia. He took a deep breath. Someone had to take charge here.

"Anything you have to tell us can wait, Pat," Tim said firmly. "You have to recover first."

"Recover? I'm. . .I'm fine." Patricia put a hand to her head. "l want to go to our camp. In the dray there's. . ." She stopped, looking toward Adam crouching beside her uncle.

Tim hesitated and then said grimly, "I'm only too happy for you to get as far away as possible from those two bushrangers."

"Bushrangers!"

"When Danny and I were making inquiries about you and Andy, we saw their wanted posters at the Bathurst police station," her father explained.

"You. . .you were making inquiries about us?" Pat asked in a dazed voice. "And bushrangers? Aren't they like highway-men or something? But we thought they were drovers."

"Droving someone else's stock probably," Danny assessed.

Patricia looked from him to her father and back again. "How, when. . . ?" She paused, closed her eyes, and swayed.

"Not now. All explanations can wait," Tim said sharply. His mouth went dry as he remembered the fear and horror that had swept through him when Jackie had reported how she had fallen in that landslide, the way the men had carted her off.

Despite Patricia's protests, Tim swung her up into his arms and started off. He heard startled objections behind him, and then John's amused voice saying gently, "May I suggest you leave her to Tim's capable care? I would say they have a few things to sort out, don't you?"

A smile touched Tim's grim face. Just one more debt he owed his father's old friend.

Tim was breathless and trembling by the time he deposited Patricia on the ground near the dray. His shortness of breath was as much due to the feel of her soft body in his arms as to the exertion needed to traverse the slope and winding track.

Patricia stared up at him from her white, strained face with an expression in her eyes he could not decipher. "You. . .you came straight here. How did you know where our camp was?"

He hesitated a moment and then shrugged. She would know soon enough anyway. "Jackie and his people have been watching your movements since not long after Andy left Blackie at Orange. Jackie led us past here so we could get close before the bushrangers spotted us."

Her eyes widened in alarm, staring at something behind him.

He turned slowly and wasn't surprised to see Andy glaring at him ferociously. The man's hands rested warningly on his guns. Andy seemed to have more of a problem with Tim touching Patricia than either her father or brother! Yet it was Andy who had ridden off with her in the dark and allowed her to be put in such danger. Andy O'Donnell definitely had not been Tim's favorite person these past days.

Tim glared right back at Andy. Then he turned and stooped to examine the bump on Patricia's head. "It's only a small cut, Pat, but I guess you will have a headache for awhile."

Without glancing back at him, Tim snapped, "Andy O'Donnell, if you think you can do anything besides wave guns around, how about getting something to help clean her up? She took a nasty tumble."

Andy didn't move. Patricia watched him over Tim's shoulder. She saw the indecision on his face, but also something like admiration for a man who would ignore his guns like that. Then Andy's gaze swept the immediate area. Her glance followed his, and she saw her father and brother standing at the edge of the camp watching them.

Tim kept brushing dirt from her face and hair, his touch gentle. He stroked her face, and she felt his hands tremble. Then he stilled. With a deep sigh, he slowly stood and confronted her uncle. Only then did he notice the Casey men. He stiffened.

Tim turned back to Andy. "Look, contrary to what you might be thinking, until Jackie told us a couple of hours ago what had happened to you both, we were only on our way here to put your minds at rest, as well as reunite a family. But we'll talk about all of that later. Right now, you'd be better off getting a drink for Pat. . .Miss Casey, " he corrected himself swiftly with a wry grin.

Andy ignored him. "You were saying you wanted to speak to me, Pat. But first, what really happened to you? How did those men get hold of you? Are you sure they didn't hurt you before I got there?" he asked ferociously.

Tim drew in a deep breath. He surveyed Pat with frantic eyes.

A deep voice behind them answered. "She fell when the ground gave way under her, O'Donnell, and Mirrang tells me they did not hurt her themselves."

Jackie stepped from the shelter of thick bushes. He ignored all of them, looking only at Tim, searching his face anxiously. Patricia stared at Jackie, seeing the aborigine's obvious concern for Tim change to anger as he studied Andy and then deliberately turned his back on her uncle.

Tim had told her many stories about Jackie. She knew Tim was as close to Jackie as the aborigine would let any white man be. Well-meaning white people had reared the orphaned boy until his longing to find his own people had made him go west. He had eventually ended up on Waverley. He was well regarded by most of the other station hands, but he had never once spoken in her presence since that day weeks ago when he had been with the other aborigines.

Andy spun around, his hands once more going to the handles of his revolvers.

Jackie continued to ignore him, instead studying Tim. "You still don't look too good, Tim," he said quietly.

Tim shrugged and asked impatiently, "Where did you get to, Jackie? We thought you would meet up with us last night. Today we waited a long time before coming on to. . ." He swallowed and then straightened his shoulders before finishing in a tight voice, "to that place where we found Father's camp."

"Sorry, Tim, I was watching this bloke." He nodded toward Andy.

Patricia's menfolk stared in fascination at the aborigine. Even though his clothes were the worse for wear and his beard and hair looked little different from other aborigines they had seen since arriving in Australia, his voice was cultured, his English perfect.

Patricia looked at Andy to see if he felt her own surprise. She frowned in sudden dismay. Was he ill? His face had lost almost all its color.

"Watching me?" Andy whispered.

Her concern increased. It wasn't illness. There was a trace of fear in Andy's voice.

Jackie merely stared at Andy impassively, all expression wiped from his face.

In a strangled voice Andy asked again, "You've been watching me?" Then he added sharply, "All day?"

Jackie shrugged. "And yesterday and the day before that."

If anything, Andy grew paler. He glanced at Patricia. A tide of red swept into his face. She frowned. That had been guilt and trepidation she'd seen on his face. Just what had he been doing that he had not wanted Jackie to see?

Suddenly she remembered. Andy had been panning for gold.

"Today I was supposed to meet up with the Waverley mob and lead them to you," Jackie continued, "but those bad men were watching you. I was concerned they would find Miss Casey too." As though Andy were the least of his concerns, Jackie turned and scowled at Tim. "But guess I left it too late. And I didn't expect to see you here as well. Miss Casey was right. You shouldn't be riding again so soon. We could have handled this."

"No doubt." Tim's voice was crisp. "But Miss Casey's welfare is my business."

Jackie stared at him a moment longer and then switched his attention to Patricia. "For many years I searched for my father's people, and I understood your need to find your brother, Miss Casey," he said with great dignity. "I saw you fall. You were fortunate not to be more seriously injured, Madam."

Patricia swallowed. "Thank. . .thank you." Her voice came out in a surprised squeak. Humor briefly touched the dark face, and she felt embarrassed heat sweep into her own. She looked away, putting a hand self-consciously to her face where it felt rather battered.

Tim crouched down again. Gently he pushed some strands of hair back from her cheek. She stared back at him.

"I'm really sorry for what happened at Waverley, Pat," Tim said softly. "They didn't mean to frighten you so badly. I want you to know I didn't blame you for either of those accidents, or. . ." His brief glance toward Andy was cool. "Or for anything else, come to that."

Patricia felt mesmerized by the way Tim touched her, the gentle expression on his face, the tenderness in his eyes. "I knew that," she said huskily.

Something flared in Tim's eyes, but then Jackie held out a cup to her with a sudden smile. As Tim took the cup from him, she smiled shyly back.

"Thank you, Jackie," she murmured. "Thank. . .thank you for everything."

He nodded and moved away.

Her eyes were drawn back to Tim's face. Her cold hand touched his warm fingers. The cup tilted, and he wrapped his hands over hers.

Someone shouted from a short distance away. Jackie melted back into the bush and a few moments later reappeared with Adam and John, leading their horses.

"Blackie," Pat murmured with relief.

Tim nodded and smiled. He hesitated, murmured, "Just rest now," and stood to meet his friends.

Tears filled Patricia's eyes as Tim reached the black horse. Blackie gave him a welcoming snicker and reached to push at his chest. The affection both had for each other was obvious. Tim patted Blackie as he engaged the others in a low conversation.

Patricia looked over at Andy. Relief mingled with regret registered on his face as he watched Tim and Blackie. Andy noticed her watching him and came swiftly to her.

"I'm glad Blackie made it to Waverley okay. He's some horse," he muttered. "Are you really okay, Girl?"

She nodded. "Andy, you. . .you should. . ."

He raised a hand and she stopped. "I know what I should do," he said briefly and started toward the three Waverley men, who were still talking quietly a little distance away.

Jackie, with the assistance of Danny and Michael, led the horses away. Patricia smiled. No doubt her family was very curious about this aborigine.

Patricia saw Andy reach the other men. As they turned toward him, she saw tension on Tim's face. He glanced briefly back at her and then scowled at Andy as the man began to speak. They were too far away for her to hear what Andy was saying, but she knew she should be there with him. She struggled to her feet. For a moment, dizziness returned, but she started toward the group of men, planting one foot carefully in front of the other.

Whatever Andy was saying had all three men staring at him

intently. Not even Tim looked her way until she was close enough to hear Andy say, "And so, if you will forgive and forget this whole sorry mess and let us be on our way, I'll let you have the gold and show you where I found it."

She gasped. Andy swung around and stared tensely at her.

"Andy, haven't you realized yet what kind of people these are? They don't mean any harm to us," she cried indignantly. "And from what Tim has told me about their being Christians, they won't be bribed anyway!"

Andy snapped, "Who said anything about a bribe? We owe for our supplies as well as any inconvenience." Then he gave a hard laugh. "Anyway, I've never yet met a man who isn't interested in gold!"

"And I doubt you ever will," Adam said bluntly. A slight smile lit his eyes. "But there is a difference between an interest in gold—especially when it seems to be so close to where one lives—and the priority some folk give it. Many things are much more precious than gold."

Tim's head went up.

Suddenly Patricia remembered him telling her his father had whispered something about that, about Jesus being more precious than gold. Could it be possible. . . ?

"At the moment," Adam continued, "our main priority is to set up our camp here with yours before dark and let you both recover from your ordeal. Then we can have this talk about gold," he finished firmly, "and all that has happened."

He hesitated and looked at John. "I believe John also has something for Tim that perhaps should not wait until we are back at Waverley?"

Tim frowned, looking from one to the other as John grinned happily back at Adam and said, "Exactly what I was thinking, Mate, but later."

Patricia watched the confusion on Andy's face as he stared at them all.

"Come on, Andy," Adam said with a smile in his voice. "By now we'll need to rescue Jackie from two curious Irishmen.

Jackie and Mirrang are going to stay at our trussed-up prisoners' camp to keep an eye on them for us until morning. Unfortunately it's too late now to take them to the police." His face darkened. "But tomorrow will be another story."

thirteen

That was the signal for all except Patricia to get busy. Despite her protests, she was made to watch as, in a remarkably short space of time, canvas shelters were erected and a neat camp set up. Patricia could not help smiling at the amazed looks the three Irishmen gave each other as they found themselves working side by side with Lord John Farnley. Obviously, he was no stranger to work or to setting up a camp. He helped gather firewood, started a roaring fire, and trudged up from the Turon River with buckets of water to heat so that Patricia and Andy could bathe away their ordeal.

John teasingly told the Irishmen to look out for Adam. "Now I warn you," he said, eyes twinkling, "don't let this bloke near the cooking pots. He's hopeless. You should have seen that first meal Timothy Hardy and I ever had with him around a campfire just west of the Blue Mountains." Then John proceeded to prepare a nourishing meal for them all.

Much later around the campfire, Patricia was pleased when Tim managed to get Adam and John to tell more stories about his father. Patricia could see by the look of delight on Adam's face that he realized the significance of Tim's eagerness to hear about Timothy Hardy. It was as though that deep well of pain Tim had kept hidden for so long was finally open to God's healing power. Even though Tim must have heard many times before the stories about how his father and John had first met Adam, he listened now with wonder and thoughtfulness, especially when the men described how Tim's father had so fervently shared his faith and helped them grow in their commitment to Christ.

Patricia was fascinated to hear Adam describe how he had taken the blame for his weaker brother's crime and then tell a little more of his own hardships until he had been assigned to George Waverley. Elizabeth's father had come from the dark slums of London and been deservedly imprisoned for his crimes; but after serving his sentence, he prospered as a pastoralist. He ended up treating Adam as he own son, even leaving the newly acquired Stevens Downs to him in his will. Not long after that, John Martin and Timothy Hardy had entered Adam's life.

Stories about Elizabeth as a young girl clearly delighted her husband. John reciprocated with stories about his own upbringing by his mother's family in Spain, his journey to England to find his father, and his new life with Elizabeth at the ancestral home of the Farnleys in far-off Yorkshire. John's voice deepened with affection as he told other stories about Tim's father. Inevitably the conversation turned again to how Timothy Hardy had shown first John and then Adam through his life and his knowledge of Scripture that a personal relationship with God was possible because of Jesus taking the punishment for their sins on the cross.

During this time, Patricia's father had been very quiet, but when John and Adam at last fell silent, staring into the fading campfire and remembering their dear friend, Michael Casey said softly, "My Mary used to talk like that about God."

Andy moved restlessly but didn't say anything.

It was Danny who whispered harshly, "But can God forgive a man who kills someone, especially a soldier who shoots a small child, even if it was unintentionally?"

Patricia saw the look of compassion on her father's face as he looked at his son. Hope flared. If Danny had been able to tell Pa everything, including his dreadful experience in the battle against the Mexican army at El Brazito, perhaps he was on the road to healing those hidden wounds in his soul.

She closed her eyes, remembering that morning when she had promised Danny to keep his secret. Perhaps if the letter telling them Danny had been reported missing, believed killed in action had arrived first and she had seen Pa's agony at the news, she would never have made that promise.

For when Danny had approached the house after her father had left for the day, she had not even recognized him until he spoke. There was little of the Danny she had known in the gray-faced, exhausted man who had stared at her from haunted eyes that had seen too much horror. After he had told her he was a deserter, she had promised not to tell Pa on the condition that Danny keep two promises. The first had been to never leave California without getting word to her somehow. That promise he had kept and was why she had followed him to Australia.

Patricia looked at her brother sadly. Remembering his clenched jaw and the denial covering his face when she had raced to her bedroom that day and returned with a familiar book, she doubted Danny had kept his other promise. But Patricia had said it anyway. "I want you to read this from cover to cover." She had cleared her throat and lovingly stroked the cover of their mother's well-used Bible.

At first Danny had refused, his face growing more bitter and angry. "You don't understand," he had said at last in a tortured voice. "I not only hate myself for running away, but my hands are stained by too much blood to even touch Ma's Bible!"

Patricia had waited in horrified silence, and at last Danny had whispered, "At Christmas we defeated a Mexican army at El Brazito. The very day Jesus was born, this little girl. . ."

Patricia shuddered at the memory of the horrors that had poured out of her brother. Somehow she had persuaded him to let her slip the precious book in his saddlebag.

"Yeah." Andy's cynical tones brought her back to the present. "And what about a gunfighter forced to kill some stupid man who wants to prove he can draw faster? And he only in that wild country because of what was done to his father!"

"Thought that had been eatin' at you all these years," Patricia's father muttered. He swallowed and added softly, "Mary told you and told you all you had to do was repent, like in throw those guns away and tell God how sorry you are and ask His forgiveness. Then He would help you forgive too."

Her eyes misty, Patricia looked at these three men she loved so much. "Tim has been telling me some things his parents taught him from the Bible, especially about forgiveness," she said softly. "I guess they must be what Ma believed too."

Adam and John glanced at each other and then looked at Tim with delight and affection. Considerable relief showed in Adam's face as he murmured, "You've found your way again."

Tim smiled at them a little self-consciously. Then quietly, with unmistakable conviction ringing in his voice, he said simply, "One of the things I remember Father telling me was from the letter the apostle Paul wrote to Timothy. Paul had been responsible for the death of many Christians before his own conversion to Christ. He called himself the 'chief of sinners,' so there is no doubt in my mind God can and will forgive every single thing—except not putting your trust in Christ's death, burial, and resurrection for us."

Joy shone from him as he added softly, "Because of Jesus, I am certain I'm going to see my dear father again."

Danny stared down at his tightly clenched hands. Patricia's heart ached for him. He had a long way to go before he could let God heal him of his grief, anger, and self-loathing. And she knew only too well that real, lasting peace and relief from all burdens could only come from the hands of God.

Andy stood up abruptly and strode off into the darkness.

Patricia stared anxiously after him. Tears had glistened in his eyes. She hesitated, wanting to go after him, but looked back in time to see Tim nodding at John. Immediately John stood and followed Andy.

Tim smiled at her and said softly, "John will be given what to say to help Andy." He paused and looked at Adam sadly. "I've had to do a lot of talking to God myself lately. When I let Father's death stop me from reading the Bible, praying, and having fellowship with other believers, I let my own faith slide badly. I've come to realize that instead of having my own faith in Christ, I was relying first on Father's faith and then yours. I've asked God's forgiveness, but Adam, I know how much my attitude these last few years has hurt and worried you and dear Kate, and I am so very sorry."

Adam beamed at him. "That dear wife of mine, as well as my perceptive old friend Elizabeth, have already assured me they were certain you were on the way back to a close relationship with Jesus."

Patricia was battling tears herself, feeling anguish for her family. She saw Adam look from Danny's tense figure to her before he added gently, "And now I think we've talked far too long. We all—especially Patricia, judging by her pale face— need a good sleep before our journey home tomorrow."

Patricia was delighted he had called her by her name and even more relieved when he smiled at her. She glanced at Tim. The look of disappointment and frustration on his face echoed her own. She longed to be alone with him, to talk about all that had happened, but Adam Stevens was right. She felt almost sick with exhaustion, and it was best to leave such conversations for a new day.

Before John and Andy returned and the others had even settled, Patricia fell into an exhausted sleep despite her aches and pains. But she woke before the sun peeped over the hills and tall gums. As she swiftly dressed, no one else stirred. She pulled on her thick coat and quietly left the campsite.

Tim watched Patricia until she was out of sight before stretching his stiff body and getting up. He had been longing to be alone with Pat. Glancing around, he was thankful no one else seemed awake. This was a good opportunity.

His mind had seethed long into the night, wondering how best to say all that was in his heart to the woman he loved. Yesterday had decided him. Despite all the difficulties that presented themselves with his lack of financial means and her family's demands on her, somehow there just had to be a future together for them.

If this was what God wanted for them both.

If Patricia loved him enough to work through the obstacles.

Tim had pretended to be asleep when John and Andy had at last returned the evening before, but John had given Tim a pat on the shoulder as he passed. When Tim had raised his head slightly, John's smile and thumbs-up sign made him sag with relief. Andy would be all right. That was one thing less to worry about.

Tim set those thoughts aside as he followed the path Patricia had taken out of the camp. He found her sitting on a rock near the water's edge. Behind her the water trickled gently over the riverbed that held even more of that precious metal men so hungered to find. She was studying the sloping cliff a little upstream and farther back from where their camp nestled.

A kookaburra in a high gum tree started laughing, giving warning of an intruder. Patricia turned her head swiftly and saw Tim. For a long moment, neither moved.

Then she gracefully uncurled, stood up, and held out her hand to him. "Why, Tim, I was just wishing you were here." Gladness rang in her voice, and he hurried to her.

Her words ran over each other in her eagerness to continue. "No, not wishing, I was praying God would send you. And He did! He answered my prayers *again*." Wonder filled her voice.

Tim gave a low laugh and said teasingly, "So I told you many times during those glorious hours we talked. God always hears and answers His children. It's only when my faith has been right down, when He hasn't given me quite the answers I've wanted, or when I've been away from Him that I thought He didn't hear me."

She nodded in agreement. "They were glorious hours for me too," she murmured a shade wistfully.

Patricia's smile made Tim catch his breath. Words he had not intended burst from him. "Marry me, Pat, my darling?"

Wonder filled her eyes, then a hint of shyness. Suddenly her whole face radiated such a wealth of feeling, it seemed perfectly natural for them to be in each others' arms. The kiss that followed left them breathless and trembling. The murmured words of love and commitment to each other that also followed left them in awe and wonder at the gift that was being given to them.

When they at last drew a little apart, Tim looked at Patricia and tried his best to be sensible when all sense seemed to have fled. He took a deep breath. "Oh, my darling, we have so much to discuss, to decide. I was going to talk first about where we might be able to live, what work I will be able to get. I am only a poor man and have nothing to offer you," he said in a concerned voice. "I don't know what your father will think."

"Perhaps you should be more worried about what Andy and his guns think!"

Tim shared a smile with her. "I'm sure the Lord's already sorting out your dear uncle," he retorted. Then he frowned. "But there is Danny. You love your brother so much you came all this way to find him, and it's obvious he still needs you. As wonderful as Adam and Kate have been, the fact remains that I only have the wages I earn working for them and no home of my own. From what you have said, your ranch is not big enough to support all of us and—"

Her husky laugh stopped him. "Why, Mr. Hardy, worrying about all this! I thought we had just decided the most important thing. You asked me to marry you, and I've said yes!"

Patricia's face sobered a little when Tim just kept staring at her. He was very serious about all these things he perceived to be problems. Patricia sighed. "I know only too well that men can get strange notions in their heads at times." She took a deep breath, and he thought he heard her murmur, "Here's where I stretch this newfound faith in You, Lord, even further still."

Decisively, she stated clearly, "If this is what God wants for us, we are going to be together, Tim dear. Nothing is going to stop us. Everything will work out."

He felt his tension begin to fade. "Yes," he said simply. Faith swept through him, around him, almost overwhelming him with excitement. "Oh, my darling, you are perfectly right! God is in control of every detail, isn't He?"

Patricia's eyes suddenly widened. "I forgot," she said with wonder in her voice and on her face, "I had actually forgotten until this moment the main reason why I've been praying God would bring you to me this morning." She started to chuckle joyously. "Why, discovering you love me as much as I love you drove it all from my head. And this is part of God's provision for us."

Tim stared at her in confusion.

Urgently she exclaimed, "There is something I must show you. Quickly." Before Tim could speak, she had caught his hand and started tugging him upstream toward the cliff and that cave.

Tim loved the strong clasp of her hand in his and prayed again, as he had so many times since her disappearance, that somehow they could have a future together. Even though he was the son of a convict with no money of his own, and she with a family and home she loved so far away across the oceans, somehow God *could* work it all out.

He was so bemused by her, so full of all that had happened, that it was only when she stopped and looked at him sympathetically that he suddenly realized where they were.

"Tim, am I right in thinking this was where you told me you found your father?" she asked gently.

He stood very still. Suddenly he realized the deep anguish, the fear of this place that had haunted his dreams for so many years was gone. In this very place, Timothy Hardy had gone home to be with the Lord he loved, and one day they would be united where there was no more pain, no tears.

Tim looked up. His eyes widened. A hiss of surprised breath escaped him.

Patricia read his expression accurately. "You didn't know the cross was there? Then who. . . ?"

"I put it there."

They spun around. Jackie had slipped from the shadows cast by the weak, early morning sun now rising in all its splendor on a glorious summer's day. He smiled gently at their startled faces and said quietly, "I thought your father would have liked a cross above where he died to remind people of the One he always spoke of. He must have managed to drag himself quite a distance. His tracks showed he was injured in that landslide."

"Jackie. . . ," Tim whispered.

A dark finger pointed up to the piles of rock and dirt Patricia had scrambled over to the cave the morning before. "That slide was much bigger than the one you found yourself in yesterday, Miss Casey." Jackie paused and looked sadly at Tim. "All those years ago I thought it best to leave what I found in the cave."

A multitude of confusing emotions tore at Tim.

Patricia gasped.

Jackie nodded at her. "I returned yesterday and saw your tracks up there. I, too, looked and read what he wrote." He hesitated. "Perhaps I was wrong to leave it where Mr. Hardy had hidden it." He shrugged and watched the dawning of wonder, of comprehension and hope sweeping through Tim. "But at least now you are old enough, strong enough to know better what to do with his legacy as he would have wished."

Before either could gather their scattered wits, Jackie turned and disappeared silently and unobtrusively back into the bush in that timeless manner of his ancestors.

Tim found his voice. "Father. . .he had been up there? Can it. . .can it be Mother's box? The box Father insisted I find?" His voice rose in excited wonder as he stared at Patricia.

Patricia searched Tim's dazed eyes, trying to read what this discovery might mean to him. After all that John and Adam had said about Timothy Hardy last night and the wonder of the time she had spent in the Lord's presence that very morning, she now understood a little more the thinking behind that letter that Timothy Hardy had written to his son.

At last she nodded. "You. . .you never told me about any box, but there is one, a very old, metal box. I found it up there not long before those drovers came. It was only after I opened it and read the letter that I realized it must be something of your father's. The letter mentioned your name as well—"

Tim did not wait to hear more. Patricia watched him climb toward the cave until he had disappeared from her sight up the cliff. She hesitated but decided not to follow him. This moment belonged to Tim and his beloved father. He would find the box easily enough once his eyes became used to the darkness of the small cave.

It was not a very long wait, not as long as she had expected before Tim was striding slowly toward her, the box in his arms. By the time he reached where she had been waiting for him, praying for him, he was staggering a little under the weight of it.

Tim carefully, almost reverently, placed the box on the ground before staring from it to her. His eyes were filled with moisture, but Patricia knew she would never forget the expression of joy, of wonder in them as he sank to the ground.

She knelt down beside him. "You. . .you haven't opened it yet," she whispered, knowing with a sense of awe that he had wanted to share that moment with her.

He shook his head and then took a deep breath and very slowly opened the box. Silently he stared at its contents, several large, dirty bags, each one carefully tied at the top. And a large envelope.

It was the last he reached for, extracting the faded, yellow piece of paper it contained. He glanced up at Patricia one more time and then started to read. When he had finished, he was very still. He reached to untie one of the bags.

Sunlight reflected off gleaming yellow.

At long last Tim looked up, searching her face. He looked completely dazed, bewildered. Tears slowly trickled down his face. Patricia put her hand into his and clasped it tightly.

Hoarsely, he whispered, "You. . .you read Father's letter?"

She nodded apologetically. "I–I'm sorry," she whispered back. "I thought it might give me some idea of the owner, what it was doing there. It wasn't until the very end when he called you 'my dearest Tim,' that I realized the author must be your father."

He was silent, staring at her. Color started to wash back into his pale cheeks. He began to quote, "My dearest Tim, something has compelled me to write this letter. I know not why because this is my last time here, my last search for this gold and. . ." Tim choked, and he looked away.

Patricia waited for him to compose himself. She knew what he was thinking. God must have prompted Timothy Hardy to write that letter.

At last Tim murmured sadly, "He. . .he accidentally found gold here that first year after Mother died and came this way every time afterward when he made the trip to Waverley. Pa intended to collect his hoard when he returned that last time to take me home and. . .and hoped it would be enough to send me to Sydney, to give me a decent education, to give me the start in the world he never had. Enough!" Angrily he added, "And all the time Kate and Adam had already made provisions and now. . ."

His head swung swiftly around and excitement started to chase away the tears and any hint of sadness. "There probably isn't enough there," he began hesitantly, then his voice began to rise with his excitement, "just enough to buy a few merino sheep to start with, but. . .oh Pat, Darling, at least it *will* be a start for us."

"Tim," Patricia said a little nervously, "there's something I haven't told you. When you first saw me, the main reason I was so, so. . ."

His eyes twinkled briefly as he tried to help her faltering words. "So stupid as to shoot me?"

She didn't smile back, just nodded. "I–I had just been washing some river dirt and found gold. Andy didn't even know until later. Apparently when we were on the way to Waverley, he found it where I had hidden it."

Tim's eyes burned into her own. He opened his mouth to speak, but a voice hailed them. They both jumped to their feet. Impatience at the interruption covered their faces as they watched John walking toward them.

"I am sorry to interrupt you." A sympathetic smile touched them both but faded completely as he held out a large envelope to Tim. "I believe that before you two talk, you should know something, Tim. Adam picked this up in Bathurst. We were going to give it to you later, but guessing how things are with—"

He stopped, his eyes widening as he saw what was on the ground. "That's Molly's box! But I thought Adam said. . ." Brilliant eyes searched first Tim's face and then Patricia's. "You can tell me later," he said hurriedly. "I can see that I have indeed interrupted you at the wrong moment."

He hesitated and thrust the envelope at Tim. The touch of diffidence and unusual uncertainty in John made Tim stiffen in sudden apprehension. He took the envelope, staring from it back to his father's old friend.

"Open it, Tim, my dear fellow. Adam and I. . ." John cleared his throat and said swiftly, "We both know how much you always longed to go back to your old home. This was something we were planning to do for your father before he died. Afterwards, Adam thought it best. . .Well, anyway, we. . .we all love you and know this would please that great man, your dear father, who, in sharing his faith, gave us both the greatest gift in all the world, Jesus Christ."

Emotion thickened the tall man's voice, making his slight Spanish accent far more noticeable. He started to turn away and then paused, saying swiftly to Patricia, "And perhaps you should know that your father and brother have been talking to us about the possibility of staying on here in Australia instead of returning to California." His face lit with skeptical amusement. "At the moment they have joined with Andy in teaching us how to prospect for gold."

He moved off again, tossing over his shoulder, "There are more plans to help you both get a start, but we'll talk after you two have rejoined us. God be with you both!"

The two young people stared after him and then at each other. Tim looked down at the envelope. It just had his name on it and the words, "The trial of your faith, being much more precious than of gold that perisheth."

He caught his breath. "Patricia," he cried out, "these refer to the last words Father spoke to me, the words he had written in that letter in case, as he put it, 'anything should happen to me before I speak to you about the contents of this box.' And now this. . ." His hands were shaking as well as his voice.

"Open it, Tim." Patricia's soft voice was full of understanding at the turmoil he was going through.

Tim looked at Pat, loving her deeply. She had lived near the California gold fields. She would know far better than he how many long hours Timothy Hardy must have spent along the Turon River washing pan after pan to find the alluvial gold he had so carefully hidden in the box for his son's future. She had read the letter that told of his father's deep love for him, the letter Timothy Hardy had written telling of his hopes, his dreams. She knew, too, the risks he had taken in this isolated place, the ultimate cost his father had paid for being so foolish as to put so much importance in mere gold.

The eyes of the woman Tim loved were full of compassion and a love that would last a lifetime. His heart leaped with thankfulness that he was not alone, that at this moment he had this wonderful woman with him.

God's timing was perfect.

Tim tore his eyes from her and ripped open the packet. After a few moments, he raised his face and stared blindly at Patricia.

Alarmed, she cried out, "Tim?" She took a step forward, and he felt her arms cradle him close. "It's all right, my darling Tim," she whispered soothingly. "Whatever it is, God is in control."

He gave a broken, bewildered gasp and held her tightly for one more blissful moment. "Oh, Patty, Patty darling, God is doing a marvelous job of being in control. These are. . ."

He took a deep breath and pulled away slightly to show her the papers. "These are the deeds of Stevens Downs and. . ." He gulped and added in a dazed voice, "Tell me, am I dreaming or are they in my name?"

After a few moments, in a voice filled first with disbelief, then with wonder, Patricia read the accompanying note out loud.

Dear Tim,

 Between the four of us, Adam, Kate, Elizabeth, and me, we have more wealth than we know what to do with. When he realized how much you still love Stevens Downs, Adam often bitterly regretted selling it. When recently it came up for sale again, we shared in buying Adam's old property back for you.

Patricia paused. Delight tinted her face.

Tim looked over her shoulder at the note. His arms slid around her, holding her to him as he finished reading the rest. A few more words had been added in Adam's handwriting.

As he read it out loud, he held Patricia close, smiling with joy at his friend and mentor's perception, his mischievous way of letting them know they all approved of Tim's choice of a life's partner.

 If you have any doubts about accepting this expression of our love for you, Patricia and you may consider this as our wedding gift to you both!

epilogue

In 1851, Australia became engulfed by gold fever both in New South Wales and Victoria. On February 12 of that year, Edward Hargraves found a few specks of alluvial gold in Lewis Ponds Creek. He later claimed the amount was much greater, and this claim helped entitle him to be acknowledged as the first discoverer of payable gold in Australia. His partners, John Lister and William Tom, hotly disputed his claim for years, until in 1891 a select committee of the Legislative Assembly found in their favor.

In reality, on April 7, 1851, while Hargraves was away, William Tom went down to the Lewis Ponds Creek to get some water and noticed a glint. The heart-shaped nugget he picked up weighed about half an ounce. He and Lister quickly found several ounces of gold. The place was named Ophir. A report in the Bathurst *Free Press* on May 17 of that year told of the "complete mental madness that seemed to have seized almost every member of the community."

Although alluvial gold would be found all along the Turon River and provide Patricia's family means to start their new life in Australia, the newspaper's report of Tom and Lister's discovery failed to excite the residents of Waverley more than their own activities that week. Waverley homestead had been a hive of joyful industry for many days, and it sparkled from top to bottom. Not a stray leaf or dead blossom was allowed to mar the perfection of the garden where the late autumn roses still bloomed.

Adding to the excitement was the arrival from South Australia of the Reverend William Garrett and his wife, Beth, who was Kate and John's stepsister, with their family for the wedding. And of course, a few days before the special event,

Tim, Adam, and John along with Patricia's three menfolk returned from working at Stevens Downs. At Harold Garrett's shout from his perch in the old gum tree, Elizabeth and Kate were not far behind Patricia as she rushed outside to greet the six men. William and Beth stood on the verandah with their arms unfashionably around each other's waists as they waited for the excited kisses and hugs to be finished between Adam and Kate, John and Elizabeth. The three couples all turned and beamed at the squeals of the bride-to-be as she was swung up and whirled around by an excited Tim Hardy.

But at last the great day had arrived.

Seeing Tim look so full of love and pride as Patricia came down the garden aisle on her father's arm, Lord John Farnley felt his heart ache that his old friends, Timothy and Molly Hardy, were not there to witness this moment. But then the glowing bride, her love for Tim shining in her brilliant eyes, clasped her bridegroom's hand and the radiant young couple turned eagerly to face William Garrett.

Kate's eyes were moist, but it was Elizabeth who had the happy tears sliding down her cheeks as she witnessed the marriage ceremony. John slipped his hand into hers, and she clung tightly to him as they both remembered a dismal day when they had first seen each other and the boy Tim. The day when it had all begun beside a grim ship waiting to sail up the River Thames. They smiled at each other, their faces alight with joy.

Perhaps John summed it all up when he whispered, "God has blessed us so richly, and I know that Timothy Hardy would not have been at all surprised that the Lord he loved and trusted has worked it all out so very, very well."

A Letter To Our Readers

Dear Reader:

In order that we might better contribute to your reading enjoyment, we would appreciate your taking a few minutes to respond to the following questions. We welcome your comments and read each form and letter we receive. When completed, please return to the following:

Rebecca Germany, Fiction Editor
Heartsong Presents
PO Box 719
Uhrichsville, Ohio 44683

1. Did you enjoy reading *Great Southland Gold* by Mary Hawkins?

   ❏ Very much! I would like to see more books by this author!

   ❏ Moderately. I would have enjoyed it more if

   _____

   _____

2. Are you a member of **Heartsong Presents**? Yes ❏ No ❏
   If no, where did you purchase this book?_____

   _____

3. How would you rate, on a scale from 1 (poor) to 5 (superior), the cover design?_____

4. On a scale from 1 (poor) to 10 (superior), please rate the following elements.

   _____ Heroine   _____ Plot

   _____ Hero   _____ Inspirational theme

   _____ Setting   _____ Secondary characters

5. These characters were special because_____
_____
_____

6. How has this book inspired your life?_____
_____
_____

7. What settings would you like to see covered in future
   Heartsong Presents books?_____
_____
_____

8. What are some inspirational themes you would like to see
   treated in future books?_____
_____
_____

9. Would you be interested in reading other **Heartsong
   Presents** titles?   Yes ❑   No ❑

10. Please check your age range:
    ❑ Under 18   ❑ 18-24   ❑ 25-34
    ❑ 35-45   ❑ 46-55   ❑ Over 55

Name _____
Occupation _____
Address _____
City _____ State _____ Zip _____
Email _____

WYOMING

Leaving the security of their Eastern cities and the comfort of their homes and families, pioneers move west—where only small forts protect them from the vast wilderness. Men join the military to defend the frontier, while their women support them—striving to keep families together no matter what the hardship.

Discover love, faith, and adventure in the forts of frontier Wyoming.

Titles by Colleen Coble
Where Leads the Heart
Plains of Promise
The Heart Answers
To Love a Stranger

paperback, 352 pages, 5 ³⁄₁₆" x 8"

❤ ❤ ❤ ❤ ❤ ❤ ❤ ❤ ❤ ❤ ❤ ❤ ❤ ❤ ❤ ❤ ❤

Please send me _____ copies of *Wyoming*. I am enclosing $6.97 for each.
(Please add $2.00 to cover postage and handling per order. OH add 6% tax.)

Send check or money order, no cash or C.O.D.s please.

Name_____

Address _____

City, State, Zip _____

To place a credit card order, call 1-800-847-8270.
Send to: Heartsong Presents Reader Service, PO Box 721, Uhrichsville, OH 44683

❤ ❤ ❤ ❤ ❤ ❤ ❤ ❤ ❤ ❤ ❤ ❤ ❤ ❤ ❤ ❤ ❤

·········Presents·········